Dear diary: the Deanna Dixon story 2©

C. WILSON

Dear Diary: The Deanna Dixon Story 2

Copyright© 2019 C. WILSON

<u>DEDICATION</u>

This one goes to all of my readers that have been asking for part 2. I'm sorry that I made you wait this long and going forward I promise to never let it happen again. Thank you for staying on my back for this book.

Thank you all.

With Love,

C. Wilson

Dear Diary,

      I had to go and get a whole new damn book because I misplaced my last one. I pray that I didn't just leave it lying around the house. Nana would flip her damn lid if she read anything out of it. Ughh! I need to be more careful with this one. A piece of me wanted to get those cute little ones that have a lock on them, but that's too childish. I'm out here doing grown woman stuff, so I don't need a kiddy ass book. Plus, totting around them little pink feathered looking things with the lock on them just looks like you're writing down secrets. For right now, I'll just stick to my composition notebook. After I fill this bad boy up, I think that my writing days are over though. Jotting down every little thing is starting to become risky…

September 4th, 2007

The first day back to school really dragged today. I had so much on my mind that I really couldn't even focus. Maybe the immature in me dragged the situation out with King, but I just can't seem to shake what happened a few days ago from my brain…

I shook my leg violently up and down and tapped my pencil in my notebook. Eighth grade, finally! Except for a few other new kids, for the most part, my homeroom class was still the same students as last year just with a different teacher. Being in honors classes had its perks at times. I don't see how Amari keeps making it in my class. I'm not trynna play him or nothing. He's smart as hell but he's always fighting and getting suspended. So, I don't get how he keeps being placed in the advanced class. My cellphone vibrated in my pocket so when the teacher turned his back to write on the whiteboard, I checked my messages.

King
Tell me if I did something wrong, Lil Mama… why are you ducking me?

"He keeps texting you?" Erica broke me from my daze.

"Mmmhmmm," I grumbled as my eyes watered.

When I looked up from my phone, I saw Amari staring holes through me. His eyes looked dark. Naturally, they were the deepest shade of brown, but this glare that he was giving me was borderline demonic. I knew that he had to be pissed with me. The same way I was ducking and dodging King, I had been doing the same to him. Erica knew all about the *situation* between King and me. Every time I thought about it, I became emotional. I knew that deep down inside fucking with him was a mistake. I'm fourteen for God's sake. Besides, me feeling guilty about me doing *it* anyways, he had to go and do what he did.

Deep down inside, I prayed that my period would come at the end of the month. I think that I was worrying myself sick, literally. Ever since *it* had happened, I wasn't able to eat a thing.

"Alright everybody, it was nice meeting you all. I hope that everyone wrote down all of the books that you will need for this class. I will see you all tomorrow…"

The teacher put the top back onto his marker and then sat at his desk. I stood immediately and walked out. Erica was right on my heels.

"Deanna…"

I heard Amari calling me, but I just kept pushing forward towards the cafeteria.

***

When we made it to the lunchroom, it was like a family reunion. Of course, we all saw each other over the summer, but there's nothing like everybody seeing each other in school.

"Valetineeeeee!" I screeched as I ran at him full speed. Like always, I jumped on him, and he caught me. My summer was filled with spending time with Erica and King. So, I barely saw any of my other friends.

"What's up with you? Ya ass getting heavy. All this jumping on me is about to be dead," he said as he placed me back onto my feet.

"I've been good. I would ask you how ya summer went, but I heard the stories," I said with a smirk.

"Whatchu talking about?" he asked with a raised eyebrow.

"Word is… you out here cuffing heavy," I said as I pointed with my lips towards a girl in our school.

He twisted his mouth into a smirk before he spoke, "yea and word is you cuffing heavy too with somebody niggas don't fuck with."

I frowned instantly.

"Let me know what's up cause right now I'm blind out here," I said as I took a seat on the lunch table bench.

"You rocking with Erica's boyfriend's big brother, right?" he asked as he took a seat beside me.

"Yea, so?" my statement was drenched in curiosity.

"Well, Amari and him got beef something terrible."

When I took in his words, my thoughts started turning rapidly. *I asked Amari if he knew King, and he said no. Was Amari the 'little nigga' that he said he would shoot in the park that day?* I felt sick to my stomach as I thought back to the very first day I had met King. I looked around the lunchroom, and when I saw Amari sitting at a table with Kha, I knew that I had to go over there. I needed answers.

"Where you going?" Valentine asked me.

"I'ma be right back."

I walked over to where Amari was sitting. I didn't know what to say, especially since I hadn't spoken to him in weeks, but I needed to know what the deal was between him and King.

"Amari… can I talk to you?" I said loud enough for him to hear me.

He was eating an apple and sitting on top of the table instead of the bench. Real boss shit. This damn boy was the biggest rule breaker I had ever seen.

"Oh? Now you wanna talk, Shawty? Na, I'm good on it."

He took a bite of the red apple in his hand and then finished talking to Kha like I wasn't standing there. The pride in me wouldn't ask him to talk again. So, I was on some fuck him shit. *Somebody gone tell me what the hell is up,* I thought as I walked back to the table that Erica was sitting at.

***

The rest of the day in school, I was lost in my thoughts. I wanted answers, but I wasn't ready to talk to King just yet. By the time the last period let out, the only thing on my mind was walking to the train and getting home.

"Cheer up bestie. I'll see you tomorrow, okay?" Erica said to me as we parted ways.

Everybody that lived by the school walked one way, and the few kids that lived in other parts of Brooklyn walked the same way as me towards the C train. As I crossed the two-way street, I heard honking. I ignored it because I'm used to old heads trying to get my attention when I made my way to the train.

"Yo, Lil Mama, get yo ass in this car!"
I looked to my left and saw King in his car, leaning over towards the passenger side.

I stood still. I battled with the thought of getting in. *Na fuck that,* I kept walking towards the train as if he didn't call me. When I heard a car door close behind me, I picked up my pace. Before I knew it, my arm was being grabbed. It wasn't a hard grab, but it was firm.

"Why do I have to chase you, Lil Mama? You got me out here looking fucking crazy," he said through clenched teeth as he looked around at the environment.
Every time he was around my school, his head was always on a swivel. *What they are saying about him must be true.* I confirmed in my head as I observed his body language.

"Got youuu looking crazy? What about me?" My voice was louder than intended, but at this point, I didn't care.

"Mmm mmm, I'm not even about to play these games with you. We can talk in the car," he said as he pulled my arm towards his double-parked car.

This time I wasn't defiant because I knew that if nothing else, today, I was getting the answers that I had wanted. He opened the passenger side door for me. After taking off my bookbag, I sat in the seat. He jogged around to the driver's side and then sped down the block. The way he watched the rearview mirror made my mental knobs turn. I couldn't hold it in anymore.

"So, you got beef with one of my friends?" I asked. He glanced my way quickly and then put his attention back on the road.

"I don't beef with little niggas," came out his mouth so smoothly that it was believable.

"So, you don't know anyone named Amari?" His silence made me look his way, and the jumping of his jawline gave me my answer.

"Why did you leave me hanging to begin with? You wanna ask me about some nigga… why did you leave *yours* on mute?" he asked, completely ignoring my question and changing the subject all at the same time.

It was time for me to face the music. For two days, his calls and text went all unanswered. I'm guessing that's why he had pulled up to my school to begin with.

"You know what you did, Kingston," I rolled my eyes and then looked out the window as the scenery passed us by. I didn't realize until now that we were going to his house. I leaned up in the chair and pulled my phone from out of my pocket. It was still early, so I had a little bit of time to spare before I had to be home.

"Actually, I don't. I know the d wasn't wack. So, I don't know why you went missing on me."

He said as he tapped the steering wheel. We were stuck at a red light, and it instantly made me think about my period. *What happens if it doesn't come?* Tears welled in my eyes at the thought of possibly slipping up. *I am soooo fucking stupid! I don't even really know him like that.*

"Hello?" – he snapped his fingers in my face, breaking me from my thoughts – "what did I do?"

"What happens if I'm... if I'm... pregnant?" I said the last word in a whisper.

He chuckled, and that made me irate. I snapped my neck his way. I felt like slapping him for not taking what I was saying serious, but the fear of him crashing crossed my mind, so I kept my hands to myself.

"Honestly, Deanna, if you are, you are. I ain't rushing to be no dad or nothing but I'm not into the fashion of killing my seed either. So... that's really it," he said as he turned onto his block.

My mouth fell open. *That's really it?* His last words replayed in my head, and it pissed me all the way off. What kind of weird crap was this man on? Yes, MAN, I started to feel sick to my stomach. I'm not even fifteen yet and this eighteen-year-old is trying to change my world forever. How could he be so damn nonchalant about something as huge as a baby?

"Honestly, Kingston, if I am... I'm killing it," as soon as the words left my body, the copper taste of blood filled my mouth.

I didn't even realize that I had been slapped until my left ear started ringing. I grabbed it and held onto it because honestly, it felt like it was going to fall off.

"Whyyy?" I started to whine, but my voice stopped once he grabbed my throat.

"Why what? Why do you like playing with me? You got the answer?" he asked me as he applied more pressure to my windpipe, "I didn't think so... neither the fuck did I."
As he spoke to me, I just looked out the windshield. I prayed that somebody, anybody walking past would look in the car and save me. Like my mood, the weather outside turned gloomy fast. The clouds turned gray, and just when I felt like I couldn't breathe, he let go of me.

"Mmmm muaaaa," I cried hard as I tried to catch my breath.

"Shut up, you're gonna piss me off for real this time with all that got damn noise," his tone was even.

I put both of my hands over my mouth to silence my cries. As the tears fell down my face, cotton-ball sized raindrops hit the windshield. Without saying anything to me, he had parked into a spot, cut the engine, and then exited the car. I waited ten minutes after he had left and decided that I was going home. There was no way that I was going upstairs with *him.* I literally had to walk in the rain towards the train station because the forecast earlier didn't mention rain, so I didn't have an umbrella. As I traveled soaking wet, I made a promise to myself to cut King off by any means possible

***

When I walked into the house, I was shocked when I saw my reflection in the bathroom mirror. My left cheek was blushed red with a bruise. I was thankful that there wasn't a bruise on my neck. Our bathroom was the very first room closest to the front door. I heard the lock to the front door turning and I knew that it had to be Nana coming in. I looked down at my soaked clothes and started to strip. I needed to wash.

"Dee Dee you done wet this got damn floor up."

"I'm sorry, Nana. I got caught in the rain," I said to her as I turned on the shower water.

"Well, it's alright." I heard her say, and then I heard her footsteps walk down the hall towards the back of the house.

I took my cellphone out of my uniform pants and then sucked my teeth once I saw that it had gotten wet. I had to take the battery out of it to let it air dry. I sat the dismembered phone onto the sink and then peeled the rest of the wet clothes off me. I made sure to be careful when I pulled my shirt over my head. My neck was sore as hell.

Knock knock knock

"Girl, why is this door locked? I have to pee," Nana said eagerly.

Shit! I thought. I didn't want her to see my face.

"Uhhh, sorry, Mam' I thought that you were bringing company inside."

"Hurry up and open this door."

"Umm, okay," I said with a shaky tone.

I quickly unlocked the door and then hopped in the shower.

"Gooood Lawd, I had to go since I was in BJs."

I heard her using the bathroom and then her washing her hands.

"Flush the toilet for me when you get out. I don't want the water to change up on ya," she said just before she exited the bathroom and closed the door behind her.

Slowly I washed my body and cried. By the time I had got out of the shower, I had heard her and Mr. Harry in the living room laughing. *Good,* I thought as I breezed down the hall and cut straight into my room. By the time I had finished applying lotion to my body and put on house clothes, my phone, and the battery was dry. I popped the battery into the back and then powered it on. Twenty-two missed calls all from King. My heart beat fast in my chest like he was right in front of me or something. Now that's fear. I was terrified by calls. I could only imagine how I would feel if I was ever in front of him again. Dings went off as I received some more text messages.

King
Where did u go?

King
I know u see me calling u…

King
Plz answer me, Lil Mama…

I laid in my bed, under my covers, and read over the texts repeatedly. I cried softly, just thinking about what had occurred earlier that day. I heard Nana's voice coming closer to my room so, I closed my eyes and placed my phone under my pillow. I heard muffled voices on the other side of my door until it opened.

"Oh, she's sleeping?" I heard Mr. Harry say.

"Mmmhmmm, her ass must be tired you know kids can't get back into the schedule of school after the summer," I heard Nana say with sass.

I heard my room door close. Before faking sleep, I wasn't really tired, and then all of a sudden, I was. I welcomed the sleep because, honestly, I was exhausted. I had one hell of a day.

September 5th, 2007

Just when I think I'm done, I'm not…

I was thankful that yesterday, the first day of school, I didn't get any homework because it would have been incomplete. I was all over the place, and I hated it…

"You been zoned the fuck out all day, you good? And what happened to your face?" Erica nudged me.

We were sitting on the bleachers at gym. Brandi was hanging with some *new friends* that were new to the school and Alyssa started hanging with the kids that cut their wrist. Now it was always just Erica and me. I was hesitant to tell her what had happened to my face because I didn't want her to look at G any differently, especially if he had never put a hand on her. Although it was obvious that King had a hand problem, I wasn't too sure about his brother. The last thing that I wanted to do was change Erica's view on him.

"I had some stupid ass allergic reaction yesterday. My face was all broke out, so now it's just a little red."

I said, hoping that she would buy it. She didn't say anything, so I figured that she bought it. The only thing was once this thing turns purple and gets into the healing stage; I wouldn't know what excuse to use.

18

Like always, the boys played basketball. I spotted Shells on the sideline with Nakita in tow. He really had turned her into his girl, and the thought of it made me want to vomit. I can't believe that I had wasted my virginity on his square ass. Mentally I started to beat myself up because not long after him, I let King hit. *I'm sooo fucking stupid,* I thought to myself. Amari running up and down the court broke me from my thoughts. I just admired his skill. That is one thing that I won't take from him. He knew how to ball.

"Yo, Ah, I'm open!" Kha said as he stood at the three-point line with his arms waving in the air. Amari tossed the ball to him, and just like that Kha was successful with a three-point shot.

All of us girls on the bleachers clapped and cheered. When Amari looked to the bleachers, he made eye contact with me. Immediately I felt insecure, so I pushed my hair onto my face to try and hide the bright red mark on my cheek. I knew that today when I went home that I would have to tell Nana something. I couldn't keep sliding past her undetected. The rest of the team finished playing the game, but Amari. He headed my and Erica's way.

"Are y'all back cool again?" Erica whispered to me.

"Mmm mm, I gotta get out of here."

I rose from the bleachers, grabbed my bookbag and then started to walk down the levels towards the gym floor.

It was nothing for me to come up with something to tell Erica about my face, but I knew that Amari would read me. He was so intimating. He carried himself like an adult, and in his presence, I felt like I was in the presence of my dad or one of my uncles. Once my foot hit the gym floor, he was standing directly in front of me. A light sweat covered him. His white T-shirt stuck to his chest, and his cornrows were neat, which was a first. His braids normally looked like he got them freshly done and then asked someone to brush over it. I looked down at his forearms and noticed that he had a tattoo on the right one. He must have gotten it over the summer. *His mother lets him do anything,* I thought as I eyed him intensely — we just kind of stared at each other for a minute. His eyes went from soft to cold and evil in a split second.

"The fuck happened to your face?" he asked me as he grabbed my chin and turned it to the side so that he could examine my profile.

"Nothing," I said quickly and then pushed his hand off me.

He gritted his teeth, "you still fuck with that nigga?"

"No," I sounded uncertain, and I knew that he picked up on it.

He scoffed, "yeah, aight!"

He walked across the basketball court to the bleacher on the other side. He sat on it and then scrolled around on his phone. My phone vibrated in my pocket.

Amari

Yo! Did that nigga touch you? Yes or no?

: Leave it alone, Amari... please

Amari

Fuck no! I been was supposed to get at him... it's over now

: Smh... leave it alone

I looked at him, and when I did, his eyes were staring through my soul. *Pleaseeee,* I mouthed. He shook his head violently from left to right. *He's so damn stubborn,* I thought as I took a seat back on the bleachers. It made no sense to leave now. The jig was up. He already knew what was up. I wanted so badly to walk across the gym to ask him what the beef between him and King was to begin with but him and Kha looked like they were holding a deep conversation.

"What was that about?" Erica asked as she took a seat next to me.

This time I wasn't going to make up a story. I mentally cried as I told her everything, and I mean everything. At the end of the story, her mouth fell open.

"I just knowwwww that pretty, fake ass thug is not putting his hands on you. Deannaaaaa, now I am done with his damn brother, and I am telling Amari!" she stood from the bleachers, but I grabbed her arm and then sat her back down next to me.

"He already somewhat knows. I didn't deny it when he asked."

She remained quiet. I didn't mind the silence because there wasn't really anything to talk about. I felt a little better, knowing that my friend knew what I had been holding in for almost twenty-four hours.

"You need to be around some love. Ask your grandmother if you can spend the night at my house next weekend. There's a party, and you need to have some fun." I smiled because I really could use the night out.

"Who's party?" I asked.

"Amari's birthday party, it's going to be across the street from my house."

"In the trap looking house that we had met him and Kha in a few months ago?"

She chuckled a bit, "Yea, it's in the backyard, though." I looked across the gym at Amari and agreed to go. I missed my friend, and somehow this weekend, I'm going to get him back as that. Especially after him showing me how much he cared about me when it came to the whole King situation.

September 9th, 2007

I'm finally starting to feel like myself. My weekend was more than good. Guess what? I got my friendddd back…

I didn't have to come up with an excuse to tell Nana about the side of my face because once I told Erica the story, she took some of her mother's Avon products. She had given me some concealer and foundation that was the perfect match for my skin tone, so the bruise was easily covered. I knew that Nana would let me stay the weekend by Erica, so I wasn't afraid to ask. Like routine, I went to school on Friday with a little duffle bag filled with my clothes for the weekend. I had been ducking King's calls and text. I just prayed that he didn't pop up at my school again. If he couldn't get the hint by me ignoring him that I was done with him, then I didn't know what else would get the message to him.

After school, me, Erica, and the crowd of kids that all walked the same way towards their homes made our way down the block.

"Oh, so you staying out here this weekend?" Amari asked me as I walked the same direction as him.

"Yep,"

I kept it short because we didn't speak since the scene in the gym.

"You got plans tomorrow night?" he looked to the floor when he asked me.

I don't know if it was him getting older or the way that he was so protective over me, whatever the reason, day by day Amari was growing cuter to me.

"Yea... your birthday party," I said with a smile.

For his skin to be so dark, he blushed. A smirk appeared on his face, but then quickly it faded.

"Aight, coo, coo. So, I guess I'll see you there," he and Kha kept walking down the block while me and Erica made a left to walk to her block.

When we got there instantly, I noticed G's car.

"Is that G's car?" Erica asked as my heart fell into my stomach.

He's somewhere around here, I thought as I looked around in a panic. If G was around, that meant that King wasn't too far behind him.

"I thought you said you were done with him?" I asked Erica in a panic as I ducked behind a white van that was parked at the corner.

"I am, I don't know what he's doing here," she said as she ducked behind the van with me.

Thinking quickly, I knew that G would have no choice but to either pull off or not say anything to us if Erica's mother was outside.

"Call your moms, tell her anything to get her downstairs. His ass won't talk to us, I bet," I whispered to Erica.

"I ain't got to call her, come on. She right there bringing bags in the house."

When I looked towards Erica's apartment building, I saw that the front door was wide open and that her mother was taking grocery bags out of her truck and placing them into their yard.

"Okay, cool, let's go," I said as I stood tall.

Together, slowly we walked to her building.

"Hey Ma," Erica said once we were close enough.

"Hey y'all, come get some of these bags out this trunk and take them to the door. The boys are bringing them up."

"Boys?" I questioned as me and Erica grabbed some bags and headed for her stoop.

"You got more bags in the trunk Ms. Fowler?"

His voice halted me, and I dropped the bags I had.

"Goddamn Deanna, that was the bags with my eggs in there," I heard Erica's mom say.

My hands grew sweaty and clammy. He walked down the stairs and picked up the bags I had dropped.

"Fix ya face lil mama, tighten up. You out here shaking like you saw a ghost or some shit," he whispered for me to hear and me only.

"Don't worry Ms. Fowler, I'll go to the corner store and get you another case of eggs," he said sweetly to Erica's mom.

I heard the car trunk close, so I knew that this brief encounter with King was almost done. He just stood in front of me, staring at me. It was an awkward glare too. He looked kind of sorry. Where I looked for anger, I couldn't find any. He and G hurried to take the last load of bags upstairs, and then they stood in the yard while Erica's mom spoke to both of them.

"Kingston, you don't need to worry about getting those eggs. Thank you both for helping me with the bags. Y'all grew up to be fine young men. Tell y'all father that I said he did a wonderful job with you two," Erica's mom said as she headed into the yard with her purse on her arm.

"Come on, y'all," she said to Erica and me, "y'all can help me put away these groceries."

I sprinted up the stairs and rushed to close the building door behind me. When I looked through the glass of the door, King was still standing in the yard. He placed his hand to the side of his head with his thumb pressed against his ear, and his pinky pressed against his mouth. He signed for me to call him. *Hell fucking no,* I thought to myself as I quickly turned around and followed Erica and her mom up the stairs to their apartment.

***

The night of Amari's party is what I should be really writing about. Now that was the highlight of my weekend...

"You sure your mother is asleep for the night?" I asked Erica as I put the hoop earrings that I wasn't even supposed to have into my ears.

Nana always said that big ol hoop earrings were for the fast-tailed girls, but I loved the way they looked. With the allowance money that Mr. Harry had given me, I had got me some from the local beauty supply store.

"Yea, once she's asleep, she's sleep. Let's go," Erica said as she grabbed her house keys and then stuffed them into her front pocket.

"Make sure one of y'all phones are on ring. If she wakes up, I'll call," Quanna said as we started to exit the room.

I honestly, at times, feel bad for her. She spends all of her time in front of that damn computer. Like she's in high school, you think that she would be out enjoying herself, but nope, her weekends were filled with playing Sims and making graphics on Photoshop.

"Hey Quanna, you wanna come with us?" I asked. Erica nudged me with her elbow, she hated for her sister to go anywhere with her, and I knew that. Still, I wouldn't be me if I didn't ask anyway.

"Umm… na. I'll just sit right here on Photoshop and be y'all lookout," she said and then turned back to the computer.

Some commotion from outside erupted, so all three of us ran to the window. I was thankful that Erica's mother's room was in the back of the apartment. Had it not been, all of the noise from outside would have surely woken her up. A crowd of people was outside of the house where Amari was supposed to be having his birthday party.

"Come onnnnn Deanna. It's starting now," Erica said as she pulled me towards her room door.

"Okay, okay," I pushed her hand off my arm and then followed her out of her room.

After tiptoeing through the living room, we finally made it out of her door. When we got down the stairs and out the front door, the scene across the street drew us over there. I pulled at the crop top that I wore. With some of the money that King had given me before we stopped messing around, I used to get me some new clothes. Nana would kill me if she ever saw me in a crop top. Another thing she said was for fast-tailed girls.

"Heyyy y'all made it," Brandi said as soon as we walked into the house to make our way towards the back yard.

I rolled my eyes as she spoke. We didn't speak in the longest. Besides her finding new friends and forgetting about her old ones, she had the audacity to try and play Erica over G. Erica was down with the fake small talk, but I wasn't. So, she gave Brandi a fake hug that she so desperately needed while I breezed past and made my way towards the backyard. I wore Bermuda shorts, but still, I pulled them down at my thigh because I was uncomfortable with how they fit. Over the summer, I had grown into a little shape. Nana made sure to point it out to me every chance she got too. *That's too tight round them thighs Dee Dee.* I heard her voice in my head. I shook the disciplinal thoughts from my noggin and told myself that I was going to make the best of my night.

After walking through the house, I had finally reached the backyard. To say that it was crowded would be an understatement.

"Hey, you were just gonna leave me?" Erica came from behind me and asked.

I grabbed her arm and wrapped it with mines as I spoke, "yea, because you were being fake with that bitch, Brandi."

"Deanaaaa," she whined, "you don't like anybody," she complained.

We walked down the backyard steps to really get into the mix of the party. After dancing to a couple of songs, I was winded.

"You not thirsty?" I asked Erica as I tried to catch my breath.

"Nope... Oooooo and this is my song!" she screeched as the DJ changed the song.

I took quarter water sold it in bottles for 2 bucks
Coca-Cola came and bought it for billions, what the fuck?
Have a baby by me baby, be a millionaire
I write the check before the baby comes, who the fuck cares?

Erica jumped up and down on beat as she shook her hand like she had sunflower seeds in them.

"Ayeeee, I get money, money I got... I get it," she rapped along with 50 Cent.

"Why you not out there with ya homegirl Shawty?" I heard someone say from behind me.

I smiled because finally, the birthday boy had shown his face.

"This is her song, not mine. Hey birthday boy," I hugged Amari.

Damn, he smells good, I thought to myself and then backed away from him to take in his appearance. He wore a plain white t-shirt with some army fatigue cargo pants. On his feet, he wore a pair of Air Force ones. His braids were freshly done and wrapped around his head he had on a folded red bandana. I pointed to his head and chuckled.

"Oh? So, you a gang banger now?" I asked as I stared at the chrisom rag on his head.

"Now? I've been one. You're just now paying attention."

Kha came to Amari and whispered something in his ear that caused him to smile slightly. The smile made me want to know what Kha had just said to him, but I wouldn't dare ask.

"Yo shawty, I'ma check you later aight? Save me a dance," he started to walk away until I spoke.

"I don't just dance to anything it gotta be my song," I said with sass.

"Well, what's your favorite song?" he stopped walking away with Kha to ask me.

"That's for you to find out. So, you better tell the DJ to play it. If you don't know it, then you don't get a dance," I said with a smirk.

He smirked back, showing that crooked grill that I was secretly starting to love.

"Aight bet. I think I know what it is, so don't bullshit me either. I want my dance," he said just before he walked away.

I watched as he slowly made it through the sea of people to walk up the stairs in the backyard that led into the house.

"Well, damn Dee Dee, you on him, huh?" Erica asked me all out of breath

"Huh?"

I knew exactly what she meant, but I was going to play dumb as hell. I don't know when I started liking Amari as more than just a friend, but it was happening.

"Nothing, girl," she chuckled, "walk with me to the cooler to get a bottled water."
As we walked over to the table that had the drinks, I felt my phone vibrate in my back pocket. Instantly, I got nervous because I thought that it was Quanna calling to tell us that their mother had woken up. When I pulled my phone out of my pocket, I looked at it to see that it was nobody but King calling me.

"Nope," I mumbled to myself as Erica passed me a bottled water.

I took a huge gulp because the heat in the backyard was starting to make me feel out of it. My fresh wash and set was now starting to puff up. So, I took the rubber band that was around my wrist and used it to pull my hair up into a ponytail. Because of my curly coils, my baby hairs laid naturally on my hairline. After about an hour or two, more people started to fill into the party. I bumped into Valentine and a whole bunch of other kids from our school. Even some high schoolers from the two schools neighboring ours, came out to show Amari some love. For him to be young, he was well known.

"What the hell this girl keep looking at?" Erica asked me.

I looked to where her eyes were fixated and saw that this group of three girls was just staring at us. I turned my body to face Erica so that the group of girls couldn't read my lips.

"Is that the same girl from the park a few months ago that was massaging Amari's shoulders?" I asked.

"Mmm-hmmm, it looks like her," Erica said before she took a sip of her bottled water.

"Hmph, she's looking at us like she wanna do something. I really hope I don't have to ruin Amari's special—" I stopped speaking once I heard my song get mixed into the last one.

He knows my favorite song. I thought as I closed my eyes and listened to the lyrics…

I see you, you wit him, he ain't right but you don't trip
You stand by, while he lies, then turn right round and forgive
I can't take, to see your face wit those tears running down yo
cheeks

I looked around to try and find Amari. As I visually searched the party for him, I saw that everyone else was singing along with Trey Songz. You would have thought that he was performing live in the backyard the way these boys were out there howling.

"You're looking for me?"

I turned to my right when I heard his voice, and Amari was standing there. I just stared at him with the biggest smile on my face.

"Did I get it right?" he asked.

"Huh?"

"Did I get the song, right?" he asked again.

"Oh yea you did, come on."

I grabbed his hand and walked him into the middle of the yard.

That's where everyone was dancing and singing. Me and him two-stepped to the song. I turned around so that my back was facing him, and he found the perfect spot right behind me. *The summer did him good,* I thought to myself when I realized that he had grown a few inches.

"Get it together. You can do better. Seeing is believing, and I see what you need so, I'm gone play my position…" he sang lightly into my ear.

I learned something new about him this night. He could sing, and I mean like really sing. *Damn,* I thought as I was basically melting to his harmony. My area below the belt felt what he said. He was getting to me. I backed up closer into him only to slowly feel him rise in his cargo pants.

"Now, I just know you got me fucked up, Ah!"

I looked up and saw the same girl that was just ice grilling Erica and me.

Very gently, Amari grabbed me by my waist and moved me to the side so that he could address the situation.

"Shay, I'ma need you to either chill or get the fuck out…"

He was calm, he always was. Before I knew it, I was elbow to elbow with Erica. I guess she must have seen the situation before it started to unfold and decided to stand next to me just in case. Even though she wasn't the best fighter, she always had my back.

"I ain't going nowhere, and what you not about to do is play me in front of my friends for some little young bitch!" The girl was yelling, which drew the attention of everyone else at the party.

"Who you calling a bitch?" I jumped in immediately. Looking at the girl, I questioned how old she could have been. She was probably in high school.

"Listen, lil girl, I ain't even about to—"

"Shay, what the fuck I just said?" Amari rose his voice to cut her off.

SLAP!

When her hand left his face, the entire party got quiet. I shocked myself when I jumped on her. Nobody and I mean NOBODY was going to put hands on Amari in front of me.

"Bitch, you stupid?" I asked as I grabbed her hair and punched her in the face.

"Yo, Deanna chill!" I heard Amari say, and then I felt someone grabbing me off of her.

"You bitches better not hop in. NO ONE is jumping my best friend," I heard Erica say, but I just kept fighting.

"What the fuck, yo Kha! Kha! Snatch Erica's ass up," Amari sounded pissed.

Finally, he was able to get me off of Shay.

"Dumb ass bitch! I'm gone see you around the hood," I yelled as Amari carried me over his shoulder and out of the party.

I could see Kha carrying Erica out too.

"Stop fucking fighting all the time, damn!" Valentine yelled at me as I was getting carried out.

I was pissed because Shay had started all of this, but yet, I was the one getting escorted out of the party. Embarrassed doesn't quite fit how I felt. I guess it wasn't that bad because I was getting taken out by the birthday boy himself. As soon as Amari got me outside and placed me on my feet, he gave me an earful.

"I'm tired of tossing you over my shoulder and walking you away from fights Deanna," he wasn't yelling, but his voice was stern.

Kha and Erica had sat on the stoop to the apartment while me and Amari stood outside the gate next to a few parked cars on the block.

"She shouldn't have put her hands on you!" I don't know why I was yelling, but I was.

"First off... lower your tone. I don't do that yelling shit, and you know that. Secondly, she didn't put her hands on *you.* So, you shouldn't have put your hands on her. I didn't ask you to come and defend me."

"You shouldn't have to. I watch you defend everyone else. Who gone ride for you? Hmmm?" I tilted my head sideways and asked.

After looking up and down the block, he stepped closer to me.

"The last person to ride for me was my sister. I don't need anybody getting hurt like that ever again just for little ol' me. I ain't worth that shi—"

"I think you're worth it," I cut him off.

I never even knew that Amari had a sister, and the look of emotion in his eyes told me that I shouldn't ask about her. At least not right now. He smirked at me.

"Whatchu trynna be my ride or die or something?" he asked.

I smirked back as I closed in the minimal space that was between us. We were so close that I could smell the Winterfresh gum that he was chewing.

"I'm just trynna give out the same energy that's shown to me."

"Oh, is that right?" he asked as our noses touched.

"Mmhmm," I felt myself getting lost in him.

"Give out the same energy shown to you, huh?"

"Mmmhmm," I confirmed.

"So, if I kiss you right now, what you gone do?" he asked me as he looked deep into my eyes.

His big eyes were the softest shade of brown. They were lighter than his chocolate skin tone, and I loved it.

"I guess we just gone have to se—"

His kiss was by far the best I have gotten. He didn't even let me finish my statement. He just went straight into it, and of course, I was a willing participant and kissed him back. I didn't realize that we were tongue kissing until he grabbed the back of my head and pulled me into the kiss more. As my tongue explored his mouth, I felt the gum that he was chewing. He was so skilled in the kissing department that he never slipped and let the gum enter my mouth.

When our kiss ended, he tapped my lips gently and then backed away from me. He stared at me with those pop eyes and then smirked.

"Fix ya face shawty. It was just a kiss."

I lowered my eyebrows after his statement. I was really starting to get the hots for Amari, and it was scary. As soon as I caught my composure, a loud screeching sound erupted, and when I turned around to face the street, I saw a car speeding down the block. *That looks like King's car,* I thought to myself, but it was too dark out to tell for sure. *This nigga got me paranoid as hell. I gotta chill,* I put my hand over my chest to slow my heartbeat.

When I turned around to face Amari, I saw that his sights were focused on the street.

"Yo, go inside. I'ma hit you later aight?" The stare that was just loving was cold as ice.

"Ummm, I was hoping that we could go back into the party. I promise I won't touch ya, lil girlfriend," I said jokingly.

"Na, I'm bout to shut this shit down. Go ahead," he leaned in and kissed me on the cheek, "go inside," he said as he nodded his heard towards across the street.
Erica stood from the stoop when Amari walked back into the front yard.

"What was that aboutttt," she squealed as we crossed the street to go back into her building.

"I'll tell you later," I was lost in my thoughts.
I didn't know why Amari had suddenly changed within seconds, but I was going to get to the bottom of it.

When we finally made it back upstairs, Quanna was still in her same spot on the computer, and it was almost two in the morning. We quickly tossed on some pajamas and then sat in the window. We watched as the party all started to exit.

Damn, it took him no time to shut it down, I thought as we watched the kids all slowly walk off of the block. I heard my phone vibrate on Erica's dresser, and I damn near raced to it. I hoped that it was Amari calling or texting me.

King

"So, you fuck with lil niggas now... cool."

I read King's text over and over as my heart beat out my chest. *I knew I wasn't bugging that had to be his car.* My thoughts were killing me. Then, I felt sick to my stomach. If that was King's car, then that means that he had to see me kiss Amari. In my mind, me and King weren't together but in his... well, I don't know what he thought, but I knew that we weren't on the same page when it came to where we stood. I sat on the edge of Erica's bed and then sighed deeply. She was too busy with her head out the window to pay me any mind and Quanna's eyes were glued on the computer screen. I just knew that drama was about to come my way and the only thing that I could think about was... I didn't even know what me and Amari were.

September 30th, 2007

Two days ago, two days ago, I was supposed to get my period. I'm finally home from my weekend at Erica's and God, I hope that I'm not pregnant...

"Lift ya head up. Mr. Rose keep looking back here and shit," Amari whispered to me.

I lifted my head up from the desk and squinted my eyes. The lights in the classroom weren't helping my headache. Normally, I would have been sitting next to Erica, but ever since Amari's party my seat in class was beside him.

"Here," he shoved his notebook to me, "copy my notes."

I smiled as I took the notebook and then opened mine.

"What's wrong with you, anyway? You got your Elmo?" he asked as he tapped his desk with his mechanical pencil.

"My Elmo?"

"Yea... your lady shit, your period—"

"Mr. Gildan, there are only ten minutes left in my class. If you would like to speak during it, then you should be the one teaching," Mr. Rose interrupted him.

"My fault," Amari said, and then Mr. Rose turned back to the whiteboard.

"No… I don't have my period nosey," I whispered.

"Then what's wrong," he whispered back with his eyebrow raised.

"I don't know."

Suddenly I felt the need to throw up, so I stood from my seat and tossed my book bag over my back.

"Well, Ms. Dixon, since you are so eager, the rest of you guys are dismissed as well," Mr. Rose said to the entire class.

Behind me was the entire class. When I got into the hallway, I felt a little better. It was like I didn't even have to throw up anymore.

"You got your clothes in that book bag, right?" Erica asked me as we walked out of school.

"Yep."

"Wait, you staying out here this weekend?" Amari asked me as he walked with us.

"Yea… why?" I asked.

"Yeaaa Amari, why you wanna know?" Erica chimed in.

"Let's go to 42nd street. Me, y'all and Kha." Amari said.

I smiled because although I hated the train ride, I loved to go to 42nd street to see all of the bright lights.

"Where is Kha anyway, I haven't seen him around school," Erica asked.

"Oh, he got suspended," Amari said before changing the subject, "y'all down or what? I say we go tomorrow since it's posed to rain tonight."

I looked up at the clouds and saw that they were starting to turn gray.

"Okay, text me and let me know what time and stuff," I said to Amari just before we turned down to go to Erica's block.

When we walked into her apartment, her mother was walking out.

"Where you going, ma?" Erica asked.

"Away this weekend, I left money for takeout on the kitchen counter," she said quickly before she brushed past us with a duffle bag over her shoulder.

"Well damn, it's gonna be a boring ass night," I said to Erica as we walked into her room.

Quanna wasn't in from school yet, so me and Erica just listened to music and got some homework done.

"Ughhhh," I groaned as I held my stomach.

That damn nauseous feeling came back.

"What's wrong, Dee Dee?" Erica asked me.

"I feel like I have to throw up. It's the worst feeling."

"Oh, girl… just take some Motrin for it. I feel like that when I get my period too," Erica said nonchalantly.

I don't why, but I started to cry like a baby.

"Dee Dee, why are you crying?"

Erica came and pushed my notebook out of the way and then sat beside me.

"My period is late E. What am I going to do?"

She looked at me with this shocked facial expression.

"What you're going to do is call King. This is his responsibility too!"

She was talking like we knew for sure that I was pregnant, and I hated it. I cried harder. Her rubbing my shoulders did nothing for me.

"Here," she said softly as she handed me my phone, "let him know."

I took the phone from her and then went to my text messages. The last text was when he texted me the same day me and Amari had kissed. My thumb hovered over my phone. I didn't know what to type. He had stopped calling me for about a week, so I just knew that me reaching out would feel awkward.

"I wouldn't text if I was you. What happens if he just leaves you on read?"

She was right. If I called and he didn't answer, I could always tell myself that he didn't have service, but once my text says *sent...* there's no excuse for no response to that.

"I don't know what to say. What do I say?" I asked Erica as I held onto my phone with a vice grip.

"Well, figure it out," Erica quickly pressed the call button, and before I knew it, the phone was ringing. I held the phone to my ear with one hand and then played with the bottom of my shirt with the other.

"Hello?" his voice crippled me.

"Yo..." he sounded annoyed.

"Kingston..." I mumbled.

"Deanna..."

He never called me by my name. It was always *Lil Mama.* I was trying to read him over the phone, but I couldn't.

"Can we talk?" I asked.

Erica sat beside me with her head to mines. She was listening to everything.

"About?"

Why is he making this so hard? I thought to myself.

"Ummm... well—"

"Look, Lil Mama, it's nothing really to talk about. If little niggas are ya speed, then fuck it. I ain't about to be chasing behind you. I don't know what more you want from m—"

"Well, she's pregnant. Now what?" Erica said, jumping the gun.

I felt like slapping her in her damn face. For every minute of silence on the phone, it only added fuel to me wanting to slap her.

"Deanna…" he said calmly.

"Yes," my voice cracked because my bitch ass started to cry.

"Can you get out tonight?"

"Yea, she can. My mother is gone for the weekend," Erica said.

She was on a roll for real. When I couldn't speak, she was surely speaking for me. I assumed that King knew that I was by Erica's because I didn't have any other female friends. Well, that and because it was the weekend. I rarely stayed home on the weekends anymore.

"I'm on my way to come and get you. You're staying the night with me," he said just before he hung up on me.

"See, now y'all good again," Erica said without a care in the world.

48

"No, the fuck we are not. He just showed no emotion! What happens if he beats on me again? What happens if he doesn't let me leave tomorrow? What happens if—"

"Deanna! Snap the fuck out of it," Erica said as she shook me by the shoulders, "he's not going to do any of that because you are going to be extra sweet."

"Extra sweet for what? He's the one that fucked up, not me," I said as I folded my arms across my chest.

"You're going to be sweet because I know like you know that you can not have this baby. You're gonna need abortion money, and we both know that no one has that but him. So be sweet, butter him up and then take it from him."

"I am not about to rob King," I said dismissively.

"Well then, slap some milk stains on your shirt and call yourself a new ass momma," Erica joked as she laughed.

I didn't find it funny at all. After the talk that me and King had in the car, he already openly said that he wasn't a supporter of abortion. *Abortion? I'm not even old enough to get a damn abortion,* I thought to myself.

"I'm not old enough to get an abortion. Don't you have to be eighteen? Oh my God, my life is over!" I whined dramatically.

"Relax, Dee Dee. Quanna's birthday is in three weeks. She can take us."

Suddenly, a huge weight was lifted off of my shoulders. I had a plan. Now, all I had to do was fall through with it. I didn't know how much an abortion cost, but I knew that if I was going to take the money from King that I was going to take more than enough to cover it.

Ding

I looked down at my phone and saw that King had texted me

King
"I'm outside."

Damn, that was fast, I thought as I stood from the bed and then grabbed my bookbag. I stuffed my homework inside because I figured that I would just finish what I had started at his house.

"He's here already?" Erica asked as she walked towards her window and then looked out of it, "oh yeah, he's here. I see his car," she confirmed.

After giving her a hug, she told me to text her so that she could know that I was alright.

When I got downstairs, I jogged to his car because of the rain. Rain. It was an instant reminder of the day he had put his hands on me. I sat in the comfortable passenger seat but couldn't relax. My nerves made it feel like I was sitting on a chair filled with thorns.

"Hey Lil Mama," he said coolly as he leaned over and squeezed my thigh.

I jumped instantly.

"Whoa whoa, relax baby girl. I'll never put hands on you again. I promise. I've been meaning to apologize, but you been going MIA on a nigga," he said as he drove towards his apartment.

I decided to say nothing because honestly, I felt like I was doing figure eights on thin ice around him. He pulled onto his block, and that's when my stomach growled. The whole time me and Erica were inside, we didn't even get the chance to order something with the money that her mother had left behind.

"You hungry?" he asked me.

He must have heard my stomach growling.

"Mmmhmm," I said as I rubbed my stomach.

"Aight, let me guess you want oxtails?"

The smile that spread across my face gave him his answer.

"Aight bet. Let me try and catch Golden Krust before they close."

He drove past the spot that he was about to park in and then headed for the restaurant. After we got my food, we were in his apartment in no time.

I followed behind him to his room slowly. It had been a while since I had been to his house, and it honestly felt kind weird.

"Ohhhh shit, what's up, sis?" G said to me as he was coming out of King's room quickly.
He was looking behind me like there was supposed to be someone with me.

"Hey, bro, what's up," I responded dryly.

"Ya, girl ain't with you?" he asked as he looked over my shoulder.

"Na, it's just little ol me."

"Aw damn, aight. Let me hit her line she probably gone answer now since you fucking with this nigga again," he said as he pulled his phone out of his pocket and then walked off towards his room.

"Gerald…" King's tone was firm.

"Yo?"

"What were you doing coming out of my room?"

"I… uh, I had to get me another deodorant," – he pulled an old spice deodorant out of the pocket of his sweats – "You know you keep all the good shit in your room."

"Aight…"

King said as he held his room door open for me to walk through.

"He like *fuck with me again…* you never stopped fucking with me right, lil mama?" King asked me with a smile as soon as he closed his room door behind him.

"Right," I said with a half-smile.

I had to remember why I was there in the first place. *Be sweet, get the money and then ghost this nigga for real,* I thought to myself.

I dropped my bookbag on the floor, took off my jeans and then my shirt.

"Give me one of your shirts," I said as he slipped out of his jeans.

He tossed me a white t-shirt that swallowed my body when I put it on. After I got comfortable on his bed, he came and sat next to me with our food bags. He passed me my platter, and then I dug in. King put on Grey's Anatomy for us to watch. It was obvious that he was pulling out all of the stops to get back in my good graces. My favorite food, my favorite show. I saw what he was doing, but I wasn't going to fall for it.

"You, my person, lil mama," he said to me throwing me off guard.

"Huh?" I asked as I closed my platter. I was stuffed.

"Like this white girl and Asian chick…you're my person, aight?"

I chuckled because I knew that he had to be watching the show on his own even to say something like that. He grabbed the platter from me and then placed it on his nightstand with his platter. After getting the food out of the way, he leaned towards me and placed a kiss on my neck. It was gentle on the skin, but the wave it sent through my body was electric.

"You gone be my person, lil mama?" he whispered in my ear.

I couldn't even answer because as soon as I was about to, a gasp escaped my lips.

"Mmmmm," I hummed as he played with my area.

I don't even know when his hand got into my panties, he was so slick like that. He pushed his weight on me, causing me to lean back and lay down.

"You gone be my person, lil mama?" he asked again as he kissed my neck and played with my pearl.

"Mmm-hmmm"

"You gone have my lil person, lil mama?" he asked.

"Uhhhh, King stopppp," I whined out in pleasure as one of his fingers entered me.

"Naaaa, answer me," he licked his fingers, stood on his knees, and then ripped my panties off of me.

He looked down at me as he licked his lips.

"You listened," he said as he rubbed the top of my vagina.

I had it shaved bald, just how he requested the last time I was in his bed. I almost cut myself doing it too, but it was worth it to get his reaction.

"Uhhh, mmmmmm," I moaned out as he entered me.

"You gone have my lil person, lil mama?" he asked again as he stroked in and out.

He was persistent. I'll tell you that.

"Yessss Kingston."

"Yes, Kingston, what?"

"Yes... I'll have your baby!"

"Mmmm," he hummed as he lifted my thigh and held it in his forearm.

The deeper he dug, the more pleasure I felt. I don't know how long we were going for all I know is that when it was done, I was sore and tired. I rolled over and started to drift off into sleep, not even caring that he had repeated the same mistake that possibly got me where I was. Let's just say that if I wasn't pregnant before, I definitely am pregnant now...

October 6th, 2007

I feel so much better now. Me and King were finally in a good space. As soon as we were, it felt like it was gone. On a lighter note, my grades are still good and as far as Amari and me… man, I think I love him…

After I spent the night with King, I flopped on going to 42nd Street with Amari. I had texted him the day of, to let him know that I wasn't feeling too good. He was trying to come by Erica's to bring me some soup from the nearby Spanish restaurant, but I had lied and told him that I had already gone home. The day after the night me and King had he started to treat me like a princess. I washed and got myself together, and then he took me back to Erica's bright and early. He said he had moves to make and he didn't want to leave me in his apartment all day.

When I walked into Erica's house, I was smiling from ear to ear.

"Ooooo, yes girl, you're smiling. Did you get the money?" Erica asked me as I entered her and Quanna's bedroom. *Damn, I forgot about that damn money,* I thought to myself. I was so caught up in the moment that I had totally forgotten why I had agreed to go to his house in the first place.

"No E, I do not have the money. I just won't feel right robbing King."

"Robbing King? What the fuck are y'all stick up girls now?" Quanna interrupted.

"No, we're not, but Dee Dee needs to be if she doesn't want a baby on her hip this summer. Can you imagine starting high school as a mom? Ew," Erica said with disgust.

"A mom?" Quanna spun around in the computer chair so that she was facing us, "you pregnant?" She asked me.

"I mean, I'm late."

"How late?" Quanna was too interested in my business. Still, I responded to her because she was older. I figured that she knew way more about this stuff than I did.

"Three days now."

She chuckled, "girl bye, it's probably just stress. Some women's cycles change all the time. Now when you are a month late, then we have a problem."

I felt relieved. Finally, someone that knows what they are talking about. Erica just jumped the gun, saying that I was, and I think that King was so excited that he didn't even question the thought of me not being. *Whew,* I sighed as I played with my hands nervously.

"Oh, thank God. Well, y'all, I think I'ma go home today."

Nana had given me some cab money to get home. I was about to put it to use.

"Whyyy girl, we supposed to be mobbin' out to 42nd Street today," Erica whined like she always did.

"Yea, I know I already texted Amari this morning and told him that I don't feel good. I'm sore as shit," I confessed.

"Ohhhh, this is why you didn't rob him. You were too busy being nasty," Erica poked fun at me.

I just smiled and pulled my phone out of my pocket to call myself a cab. I read over my text messages before I did.

Amari

"Feel better, Shawty, you on my mind for real."

King

"I miss you, lil mama."

These two, I don't know what I'm going to do with them, I thought to myself as I closed out my text and then called a cab for myself. I had planned on going home and then getting ready for the school week.

***

"You feeling better?" Amari asked me.

"Not really," I groaned as I sat back in my chair.
I was tired as hell. Monday mornings always seemed to drag,
and Mr. Rose's boring math class didn't make it any better.

"Good thing is he's about to give us homework, and
then we outta here."
Amari was right after Mr. Rose gave us the homework
assignment, he dismissed the class. I stood up from my seat,
and immediately Amari pulled me to sit back down.

"What happened?" I asked as I turned to look at him.

"You don't wanna walk nowhere right now, shawty."

"And why the fuck not?" I snatched my arm from him.

"Ya Elmo came, and it's on the back on your uniform
pants," he whispered.
I looked around the classroom and saw that the rest of the
class was leaving. Everyone except for Erica, she was waiting
for me. I felt embarrassed. I just couldn't imagine how big the
stain must have looked up against my khaki pants.

"Ummmm, I said the class is dismissed. Why are y'all
still here?" Mr. Rose questioned.

"Chill out, any other time you never want us to leave.
You can head to lunch, I'll lock the classroom up," Amari said
in a dismissive way.
To my surprise, Mr. Rose grabbed his keys and then excited
the classroom.

"What y'all still sitting here for?" Erica asked as she walked over towards us.

"I caught my damn period, and it's on my clothes," I said in an embarrassed tone.

"Oooo, okay, I'll go to the main office and tell Ms. Phay that way she can call your grandmother," Erica said. She made her exit after I thanked her.

"Look, you gone have to clean ya self up, here," Amari took off his champion hoodie and then handed it to me, "tie this around your waist and then go in the bathroom and handle your shit."

I took the sweater from him and then tied it at my waist. I looked down in the seat and saw the red stain on the wooden chair.

"Fuckkk I need to—"

"You need to go handle your shit. I'll clean it up." He interrupted me.

Although I wanted to, I didn't protest because I wasn't in a position to. I was thankful that I always carried pads inside my bookbag. After quickly cleaning myself off with tissue in the girls' bathroom. I put a pad on and then rewrapped the sweater around my waist. I left the bathroom and walked back to Mr. Rose's class to see that the room was locked. I waited in the main office until Nana came for me.

In no time, she and Mr. Harry walked in and took me home.

"You okay lil slugger," Mr. Henry asked as soon as we got into the car.

"Yea I'm good, thanks for asking."
Amari saved the day for me, and I was grateful. I sent him a text letting him know how thankful I was.

Ding

Damn, that was fast, I thought as I opened my text message.

King
"How are you feeling, baby mama? :)"

I read the text but didn't even bother to respond. *Baby mama, my ass,* I thought to myself. *Thank God, my period came!* I smiled at my thoughts as Mr. Harry drove us home.

***

When we got home, I got straight in the shower. After handling my hygiene and then putting on some comfortable pajamas, I lounged around in my bed and watched some t.v. I can't remember the last time I just laid down and relaxed.

Ding

I tapped around my comforter until I reached my phone.

King

"Babbyyy mama... wyd, pretty girl?"

For some strange reason, I smiled when I read it. *He's sweet, but I'm sure he's about to be hype as hell that he's off the hook,* I thought as I texted him back.

: Aww, my period came so no more "baby mama" and nothing watching this lame play on B.E.T you?

No later than two minutes after I sent the text message, my phone started ringing. I hated talking on the phone with boys when Nana was home, but it had to have been important because when I ignored the first call, the second one came rolling in. I tried to listen to hear where Nana was in the house. When I heard Madeea's voice boom from the living room t.v, I knew that she was partaking in her afternoon ritual. Tyler Perry plays with Mr. Harry.

"Hello," I finally answered.

King's sigh made me hold my breath.

"Lil mama… why?"

"Why what?" I asked.

I was confused, but I felt like the conversation was about to get heavy, so I turned up my t.v a bit so nobody in the house would hear me.

"Why… you killed my baby Lil Mama?"

"Killed your baby what are you talking about Kingston—"

"You say you got your *period,* but we both know that you ain't want a baby by me from the start."

"Kingston, I don't even have money to do what you are accusing me of."

"Well, $500 was missing from my stash. Put it on everything that you ain't take that shit."

"I put that on my life; I didn't!"

Thank God, I didn't, I thought as I started to sweat nervously. He chuckled, and it was the creepiest thing ever.

"Aight lil mama, it's cool," he chuckled again, "it's cool lil mama… ima check you later aight?"

I didn't even get a chance to respond before he hung up in my ear. I bit my nails, a nervous thing I always do. I knew damn well that I didn't take that money, but now knowing the headache that was about to come my way, I really wish I would have.

October 17th, 2007

I normally don't find time to write during the week, but I had to today. Today was the first time that I had cut school, and to say I messed up big time is an understatement. In-between me writing, I keep walking out of one room and into another. Two people really close to me is hurt. I really pray that everything will be alright. I just knew that I should have just taken my behind to school…

"Are we going to the corner store to get some breakfast before we go into the building?" Erica asked me as we walked through the park towards the school. She would always meet me at the train and then walk with me towards the school.

"I am kinda hungry, so that's cool."
Instead of making the right on the block of the school, we kept straight to go to the corner store that was behind the school. When we walked into the store, a couple of kids from the school were getting some breakfast and then rushing off to not be late for atfirst period. Everybody always made sure to walk into the building a little earlier to leave extra time to make it through the metal detectors.

"Next… who's next to order?" the man standing in front of the grill asked.

"Can I get a bagel with cream cheese and bacon," I asked as I licked my lips.

I was hungry, but as soon as the smell from the bacon hit the grill, my hunger turned into starvation.

"Make that two," Erica added to my order.

I walked to the back of the store to one of the coolers to get myself an Arizona. Erica followed behind me.

After we got our drinks, we waited for our food to be done. The Spanish music playing in the store held an upbeat tempo that brought happiness to my mood. I was still in a funk thinking about how King had accused me of stealing from him. I still hadn't told Erica about it, and I honestly didn't think that I wanted to. I felt like in our friendship so much was always going on with me. I was tired of being the bearer of bizarre news. I was starting to feel like I never had a break in my life. Ever since meeting King, my entire world had gone to the shitter. I was constantly on this up and down ass rollercoaster, and I was starting to hate it.

"Hey, Mami... hello... your breakfast is finished, my love," the man behind the counter was bagging up me and Erica's breakfast sandwiches.

I was so lost in my thoughts that I must have zoned out. When I looked over at Erica, she was so engaged in her phone that she wasn't paying attention either. I knew that she had heard him just how I did. Her continuing to look in her phone was her telltale sign when she didn't have any money. I dug into my uniform pants pocket to grab my money that Mr. Harry had given me for the day.

I paid for our breakfast and then grabbed the bag from the man.

"Thanks, girl," Erica said with a smile.
I just smiled back. There was no need to speak about what was done. She was my girl. If she needed and I had, then she had.

"Y'all gone be late as fuck to school," I looked up and saw Amari sitting on top of a mailbox that stood on the corner.

"So are you... let's go," I said as I walked over to him.

"I'm not going today."
I hated how he looked me directly in my eyes when he spoke to me. I did the same when I spoke to people, but his big brown eyes always seem to pierce through me.

"And why not?"
I asked as I handed Erica our breakfast bag and then placed my hand on my hip.

"Today, just not a good day for me."
He looked down the street, breaking the stare that we had as we held a conversation.

"So then why are you over here by the school if you aren't going in?" I asked.

"Kha is back from his suspension. The niggas he got into it was threatening to jump him, so I walked him here."

"Okay, that was noble of you. Now bring ya ass in the school too."

I reached up and grabbed his hand. I pulled on him until his feet were planted on the concrete. Erica stood on the side and just waited for me. When I saw that Amari was not budging on going to school, I made a decision.

"Erica, go to school. If any of the teachers ask, tell that I'm sick."

She looked at me with wide eyes. I nodded my head towards the school.

"Well, I guess I'll keep Kha some company today." She said before she walked off. When she got across the street, I just looked at Amari. He wore a smirk on his face, which made me smile, and I don't even know why.

"So, today isn't a good day for you? You wanna tell me why?"

I was intrigued with knowing more about him. He was damn near the only male that I considered a best friend, and I still did not know all there was to know about him. He ignored my question and just started walking down the block.

Without saying anything else, I followed behind him. After walking five blocks down, he made a right.

"Wherever we go, we need to hurry up and get inside before Truancy comes around."
I made sure to say. Being outside after school had already started was a risk, but I trusted him so much that I didn't care where he was taking me. Something was troubling him, and I just had to know what it was. He walked to this building and walked up the three stairs that led to the front door. He pulled his keys out of his pants pocket and then unlocked the door. The apartment that we walked to was on the first floor and in the corner. He opened that door with another key from the same ring. I followed him inside, and instantly the smell of vanilla hit my nostrils.

We walked down a long hall that opened up to a living room. I grabbed the back of his hoody and pulled him to me.

"Who's house is this?" I asked.

"Amari? Es that you Papi?" a woman called out from the back.

"Si Mami es me…" he went off to speak Spanish.
I let go of his hoody and looked on in amazement. I was today years old when I learned that Amari spoke Spanish fluently. An older woman with silver hair and skin the same color as caramel toffee walked into the living room. Her eyes opened wide when she saw me standing behind him.

"Ma, this is my friend, Deanna," he said as he moved to the side.

I was hiding behind him a little. Her filled cheeks rose with a smile.

"Hola Deanna," she turned to look at Amari, "ella es bonita."

"What did she say?" I whispered to him.

"She said you're beautiful."

I instantly blushed. She looked just like Amari, just with lighter skin and lighter eyes. Amari nodded for me to sit on the nearby chair, so I did. They went back and forth with conversation for a little while before she walked into the back of the apartment.

"Your mother seems nice. Why didn't you tell me you a Puerto Rican?" I asked with a raised eyebrow as he took a seat next to me.

He laid back into the sofa and tossed his arms onto the back of the chair. With his arm behind me, I caught butterflies.

"There's other kind of Spanish people besides Puerto Ricans."

He spoke to me with his eyes closed. I looked at him and saw for the first time that despite our young ages, he was aged. I mean, I guess stress can do that. His facial hair was starting to grow. He took his hand and cupped his chin as he rubbed the sides of his face.

"Tell me why today is a bad day for you."
I was begging him. He sighed like the weight of the world was pushing down on his shoulders. He was under so much stress that I felt it. Sitting beside him on the plastic-covered floral printed couch, I felt the weight of the world too. An awkward silence fell upon us as we both just sat there. I laid my head on his shoulder and rested my eyes while I waited for him to talk. I knew that eventually, he would speak. So, I didn't rush him.

"On this day, five years ago, my sister ran away."

I lifted my head off of his shoulder. Obviously, I had heard him wrong. I chalked it up to my right ear, being covered by his shoulder.

"Huh?" I asked because I had only recently discovered that he had a sister.

"I know you heard me… she was older than me by like three years."
I knew that he hated repeated himself, so I just shut my mouth and let him talk. He chuckled, which was weird because what he was confessing to me was no laughing matter.

"You say the word was like…" I trailed off my word because I didn't want to say *like she was dead*, but it was on the tip of my tongue.

"A year after she ran away, police came to our door and told us that her body was found in the Bronx."

I put my hand over my mouth as my eyes began to water.

"I'm sorry for your los—"

"Mm mm, don't do that," he cut me off.

He finally opened his eyes, and when he did, he turned his body to face me. He cupped his hand under my chin and then wiped away the tears that had involuntarily fallen down my cheeks. Somehow, he found some way to comfort me when I should have been doing that to him.

"I came to terms with it. It's just that on this day, I like to zone out. More than anything, I stay home from school to keep an eye on my moms. She still ain't find her peace with all of this."

I looked around the apartment as he spoke. For the life of me, I couldn't understand why someone would run away. It looked like Amari's mother could keep a house. It was clean, well decorated, and even smelled good.

"Why did she run away to begin with? If you don't mind me asking?"

He sighed again. Damn, that sigh always brought pain to my heart because when he did it. You felt his pain.

"My uncle came over from Honduras and stayed with us for a bit."

He paused and then bit his bottom lip. I rubbed his shoulder to try and console him since I knew Amari opening up wasn't his strong suit. His bottom lip quivered. He blew out a sharp breath and then continued.

"My moms always been big on family. I mean huge. So, when her baby brother came to visit, she was thrilled. It took us two months to even realize that the nigga was fucking raping my sister."

Too much was being revealed at one time, and my emotions were all over the place because of it. I gasped. He looked at me and as soon as he did, I saw that tears were coming from his eyes. Just how he had done me, I cleaned his face for him.

"She left after that, huh?"

"Na," he shook his head rapidly, "she didn't leave until she confessed the shit to my moms, and she didn't believe her."

The inner me couldn't understand how he was so loving towards his mother after that.

"You and your mother seem cool, though."

"Yea, well, my sister used to lie about dumb shit all the time, but I knew that she was telling the truth with this one. It was fear in her eyes every time that bastard was around. This is why she pretty much lets me do whatever I want right now."

Something about his story was bothering me. On the day of his party, he had told me that he didn't want me defending him because the last person to defend him was his sister, and he didn't want anyone else being hurt for him. There were so many question marks. I didn't get why he felt the need to carry the burden of his sister getting hurt. In my eyes, it had nothing to do with him.

"The day of your party, you said your sister got hurt defending you. What was done to her, no one could have predicted. That has absolutely nothing to do with you." I said to him as I rubbed the back of his hand.

"But it does… when my uncle first came to visit, he wasn't supposed to stay. He ended up staying because my mother felt like I needed a father figure. She blamed the reason I got into so much trouble on the absence of my dad. So, his ass ended up staying. I was a little nigga back then, so he used to smack me around and for the smallest things. That was until my sister stepped to his ass. She went from telling him off to being as quiet as a church mouse when he came into the room. I should have known then."

He blamed himself, and for that, I felt bad for him.

"When they found my sister's body, I needed my uncle gone for good. He had vanished when the rape hit the fan, but

I just knew that he was still in the states. That's why me and ya boy don't like each other."

I raised my eyebrow at his last statement.

"My boy?" I questioned.

"Yea, King. Our beef started because back then, I reached out to him for help with finding my uncle. If anybody in the hood could have found my uncle, I knew that his father could. Man, that nigga told me that my sister got exactly what she deserved. When my pops was around, there was a beef between my dad and King's dad. I thought that shit was water under the bridge since my old man left New York but, I was proved wrong the day I stuck my neck out asking for help. I told King that I would kill him one day. Me and ya boy has been at it ever since." He said in what felt like one breath.

This had been all of the answers that I was looking for, and now they were being hurled at me. Suddenly, I got hot. I didn't know if it was the plastic from the chair, the simple fact that the living room didn't have not one fan or the fact that we were talking about King. Whatever the reason, I was burning up.

"You're sweating," he said to me as he observed me.

"I'm alright," I said as I wiped the sweat from my nose.

"No, you're not. Come on," – he stood from the sofa – "there's an air conditioner in my room."

He reached for my hand and then pulled it gently to get me standing on my feet.

"Are you gonna get in trouble for having me in your room?"

I asked as I held his hand and followed him towards the back of the apartment.

"Na, I just told you my moms let me do whatever I want, especially after everything with my sister."

"Mmm, okay."

He opened a door and then we walked in. His room was neat, which was surprising. Not because he was dirty or anything, but I always assumed that boys were messy. King's room always had clothes somewhere, and Shell's room looked a mess most the time. He seemed only to clean it when he knew that I was coming over. Amari hadn't even expected me, and his room was just naturally clean. I breathed in deeply. *It even smells clean,* I thought.

"You can sit down."

He held his hand out towards the edge of his bed. I started to take down my uniform pants, but then he interrupted me.

"The fuck you doing shorty?" he asked me with a raised eyebrow.

"It's rude to sit on someone's bed with street clothes." King had taught me that, and I guess it kind of stuck with me. Since he didn't have a chair in his room, and I wasn't going to sit on the hard the floor, I decided to come out of my khakis.

"Naaaa, where the fuck you get that from? Pull ya damn pants up and sit. It ain't like you about to be rolling round in my sheets with outside clothes on. You are only sitting on the comforter."

He closed his room door and then plopped down on the edge of his bed.

After I took off my bookbag and dropped it to the floor, I plopped down beside him. He turned on his television. I kicked off my shoes and then sat further back onto the bed. I pulled out my phone and played a game on it as he watched basketball highlights.

"Thank you."

"For what?" I asked as I looked up from my phone.

"For being here with me today."

I smiled.

"That's what best friends do."

I didn't know what we were, but naturally, the statement left my lips. There was a silence after my statement until I heard his sneakers hit the floor. I knew that he had kicked off his shoes.

He then turned to face me and made his way to the top of the bed like me. Once his back was against his headboard, he held his arm out and motioned for me to lay in his arms. After putting my phone down, I did. As he continued to watch his basketball highlights, I started to doze off. Once I was under his armpit, I kind of laid my head onto his stomach. He cupped my body with his arm and gently started to stroke my hair. If I wasn't tired before, I was definitely tired when he started playing in my hair — the night before, I didn't really get any sleep. Since the conversation with King about him accusing me of stealing his money, I had slept less. I tried to fight against my heavy lids with each blink, but it wasn't working.

"You're more than my best friend shawty," I heard him whisper before he placed a kiss onto the top of my head. I smiled inwardly and continued to play like I was already sleeping. Which didn't take too long because in no time I was out...

***

Knock, knock, knock

"Amari?"

Knock, knock, knock

I heard Amari's mother speaking Spanish on the other side of the closed door. Slowly I blinked my eyes, sat up, and looked around the room. Amari was still the same way before I went to sleep. His head was rested against his headboard, and his mouth was wide open. Lightly he snored. I had half a mind to let him sleep until I checked the time on my phone and saw that school was out. I had missed a call from Nana and five missed calls from Erica. *Fuckkkkk!* I thought as I shook the hell out of Amari.

"Wake up, wake up!"
His sleeping brown eyes that peeked open slightly fluttered. He blinked a few times before he responded to me.

"Why the fuck are you shaking me like this?"

"It's 4pm. School got let out almost two hours ago. My Nana is gonna kill me."
I jumped up from the bed and stepped into my sneakers. He sucked his teeth like he was annoyed.

"Relax, tell her you ended up staying for afterschool… duh, Deanna."
He stood from the bed and put his sneakers back on as well. *Afterschool?* I thought to myself. I didn't attend an afterschool program since I left the cheerleading squad. The only reason I

joined that, to begin with, was to have more time to spend with Shells afterschool. I didn't know if Nana would buy it, but I guess I would try it.

"What are you doing?" I asked him when I saw him pick up his house keys from his dresser and then open his room door.

His mother was still standing on the other side. She spoke to him in Spanish. He killed me how he responded to her in English. It was like he didn't want me to hear his native tongue or something.

"No ma, we not hungry. I'll be back," – he turned to me – "come on, Deanna."
We walked past his mother, and I smiled at her.

"You know you don't have to walk with me, right?" I said to him as we walked back towards the school.
He ignored me. I hated it when he did that. It was like most of the time, I was talking to myself, but I always knew that he heard me. He just rarely responded. The short walk back to the school ended, and I decided to call Erica back first. It felt like she picked up on the first ring.

"Dee Dee, where are you?"

"Standing in front of the school, Amari just walked me back from his house. I'm gonna be late getting home. Did you speak to my Nana?"

"Mr. Harry had a heart attack. She called me, and I told her that you were in study hall after school."

I placed my hand over my mouth as tears started to form in my eyes.

"Mr. Harry had a heart attack?" I repeated what she said because I couldn't believe it. Quickly I pulled myself together. "Is he okay?" I asked.

"I don't know. I just know you covered on the time you were missing. Hurry up and make it home or call her back." Erica said.

"Okay."

I said just before I ended the line. I couldn't even get much else out. My heart was racing. Mr. Harry was like a grandfather to me. I couldn't imagine anything happening to him.

Amari turned around from the street to face me.

"Get your nerves under control, shawty. Remember, she doesn't know that you know yet."

I shook my head up and down and then took a deep breath. Right when I pressed the button to call Nana, tires screeched. Me and Amari looked towards the street, and just as I was getting a clear view of King's car, I was getting knocked down to the floor.

Boom… Boom… Boom…

Amari's weight on top of me made it feel like I couldn't breathe. Or maybe I couldn't breathe. *Oh my, God, am I shot?* I quickly thought. I didn't feel any pain, but then again, I heard that you wouldn't, not in the height of the drama anyway. Amari was faced away from me, but I felt him breathing on my chest.

"Amari…" I whispered.

"Amari!" I said a little louder.

It sounded like he was talking underwater or something.

"Don't tell the cops… it was… him."

I picked my arms up and gently turned his head to face me. His teeth were stained red, and blood was coming out of his mouth.

"Oh, my God! Amari! Help!!!!!"

I couldn't push his weight off of me, so I just laid under him, screaming for help. I saw that my cellphone didn't fall too far away from me, so I grabbed it. When I looked at my screen, it was cracked, and the phone call was connected with Nana. I put the phone to my ear and heard her screaming.

"Dee Dee! Deanna! Oh Lord, DEANNA!"

"Nana, I have to call you back. I need to call 911," I said frantically.

"You tell me if you're okay first!"

"I'm... I'm fine, bu... but my friend isn't."

I was stumbling over my words.

"Are you at your school. I'm coming to you sugar."

"I'm right out front."

I managed to say before I hung up on my Nana and then placed the call to 911. After they got my location, I tried to hold small talk with Amari.

"Where does it hurt Amari?"

"Shit doesn't hurt," he coughed out.

He swore up and down that he was Teflon hard, but we both knew that wasn't true. Especially with bullets riddled in him right now.

"Where are you hit? Just keep talking, okay."

"Mmm-hmmm, and I think my shoulder and my back."

He kept coughing. The more he coughed, the more blood he coughed out. The color of the blood went from a bright red to a deep burgundy color. It didn't look good, so I knew that it must not have been good. *So, nobody is going to come out of this school!* I thought to myself. I hated my school some times. It was always gunfire around it, so I guess at this point, the staff was used to hearing it. In the distance, I heard the sirens and I felt relieved.

"Help is coming, okay? They are coming." I said to him, calmly.

"I love you, shawty."

My chin dug into my lower neck as I looked down at him. His eyes were closed, and his bottom lip was quaking.

"Mmm mmm, this what they do in the movies. A person gets shot then start confessing love na... you good, okay?"

He laughed hard as hell, which made me smile.

"Na fuck the bullets... I really love you."

I was swoon. Over and over, I silently prayed that the ambulance would hurry up.

"I love you too, Amari," I whispered.

I did. He was everything that I could want in a friend. He was solid. What was there not to love.

An EMT came up to the side of us and asked me a lot of questions back to back about what happened.

"Those two are my students. Are they okay?" I heard Mr. Rose's voice.

Nowwww somebody wanna come out the school building, I thought to myself as I rolled my eyes. They only felt safe with stepping outside because the first responders were on the scene now.

"Okay, what's your name, sir?" the EMT asked Amari.

"His name is Amari," I answered for him.

"Now, Amari, can you feel your legs?"

"No," he whispered in response.

Instantly I started crying. Now that did not sound good. I just closed my eyes and let the two EMTs do their jobs. When I felt the weight of Amari lift off of me, then I knew that they had him on the stretcher. I sat up instantly.

"Whoa lay back down brave girl, were you hit?" a police officer asked me.

I hated that he spoke to me like I was a baby, but I didn't say anything about it.

"No, I wasn't. He saved me," I cried out.

I watched the ambulance workers rush him to the back of their service truck.

"Deanna!!!" I heard my Nana scream as she ran down the block towards me.

I met her halfway and fell into her arms. Her warm kisses flooded the top of my forehead.

"Thank you, Jesus. Thank you, God," she repeated over and over between kisses.

"I need to make sure my friend is okay. Nana, he saved me."

She cupped my face and looked down into my eyes. She had fear in her eyes, and it hurt me to see it.

"Okay… officer," she called out to the same man that had asked if I was hurt.

He walked over to us, closing the space in.

"Can you tell me what hospital they are taking that boy to?"

"They are gonna take him to Brookdale."

"Okay, thank you, sir."

"May I have a word with this young lady here?" he asked Nana.

I stood under her arm and watched as they engaged in conversation.

"You may speak with my granddaughter right now, in front of me."

Nana wasn't anti-police, but in her day, she was a Black Panther. She didn't play around.

"I know right now is a trying time, but I have to ask. I just wanted to know if you remember seeing anything," he kneeled down and spoke to me.

I remembered what Amari had said. For some strange reason, he didn't want the police to know that King was responsible for the shooting, so I wasn't going to tell. Now, if he didn't pull through in the hospital, then that would be another story.

"It all happened so fast that I don't even know where the bullets had come from. I just knew that Amari knocked me to the ground and saved me. If he didn't do that, I would have been shot," I started to cry.

"Give me your card officer. She is too distraught right now for this. IF she remembers anything else, then I'll see to it that you will get called, okay?" Nana said to the officer.
He took a card out of the pocket on his shirt and handed it over to Nana.

"Thank you for your time," he said before he walked away.

As soon as we were given our privacy, Nana hugged me again. She didn't care that she was getting Amari's blood all over her.

"We need to go home so you can shower, and then we can head on over to the hospital. He's in the same hospital as Mr. Harry so we can really kill two birds with one stone."
I had to act shocked. Remember, this was all the information that I wasn't supposed to know already.

"Nana, what happened to Mr. Harry!"
I put on my best award-winning performance as I covered my mouth. She shook her head from side to side and led the way towards her parked car.

"He had a damn heart attack when we were shopping at BJs. All I wanted was some groceries, and his ass dropped."

"What is the hospital saying?" I asked.

"Well, they said it was a mild one. There's no blockage or anything like that, but they do want to keep him overnight. I'm pretty sure your friend is going to need some surgery. You'll be there by the time he's out of it."
She opened my car door for me and then I got in. *If he gets out of it,* I thought to myself as I played with the crucifix chain that was around my neck. I said a silent prayer for Amari and then kissed the cross all before Nana was able to get into the driver's seat and pull off...

January 2nd, 2008

Somewhere in-between me going back and forth to the hospital and trying to keep up with my classes, I haven't had time to write. Amari is fully recovered, and I'm so thankful for that. Because the end of the school year is right around the corner, I started taking Saturday courses at Bedford Academy to prep me for the geometry courses that I would be getting in high school. I tried my hardest to spend less time at Erica's. No one had heard a thing from King but something told me that he was just lurking in the shadows. I was thankful that he didn't know where I had lived. The only reason why I didn't worry about Erica's safety was because she told me that she and G were still in contact with one another. For the life of me, I couldn't understand why after so many years at odds, that King had decided to shoot Amari finally. I knew that it couldn't have been just solely based on little ol me. It had to be deeper than that. I didn't find out the real reasoning behind the shooting until Erica had put me up on some very much missing game.

Two weeks ago…

"Shouldn't you be with your family or something. Christmas is right around the corner."

Amari said to me as he sat up in the hospital bed. He was right. My mother was due to come back to New York any day now, but I knew that she would understand me visiting him. I was bringing him his homework so that he didn't fall behind when he finally returned to school. On top of helping him with what he was missing, I was studying for the math course that I was taking every Saturday.

"My mother knows that I come up here every day after school. She likes you without even meeting you yet. I mean, I guess she would, considering that you saved me and whatnot." Briefly, I looked up from my work to give him a smile after my comment.

He made eye contact with me and then smirked.

"You so focused. What you over there doing our work or your high school stuff."

He put on a snobbish voice like them rich people, and I laughed.

"This geometry stuff."

I sat my pencil down because I couldn't concentrate with him talking to me. That and well, the shit was hard, to be honest.

"You look stressed. Let me help you."

He offered as he held his hand out for my paper. I held the paper out for him to take, but as soon as he reached for it, I snatched the paper away.

"Boy, please. You don't know anything about geometry." I teased.

"Pshh," he made a noise with his mouth, "I know about shapes and shit."

I started cracking up laughing.

"You're annoying. You know that?" I asked him.

"So, I've been told."

His mother walking in interrupted what would have been my response. I would sit with him until she showed up. I didn't leave because I wasn't wanted or something but more so to give them their time alone together. Whenever she came to visit him, they spoke in Spanish, and I didn't know what the hell they were saying half the time. Amari had started to teach me a little Spanish, but with me being drowned in schoolwork, I couldn't learn as easily as I normally would have. As I gathered my book bag and my coat, Erica had called me. I ignored her call because I was saying bye to Amari.

"Don't just wave, come, and give me a hug. You know I get out tomorrow, so I guess I'll see you when I get back to school."

I walked over to the bed and then gave Amari a big hug at his request.

"Awww." His mother smiled and then clapped her hands as we hugged.

"Love you, shawty." He whispered in my ear.

"I love you too, Amari."

Every time I left him for the day, he always made sure to tell me that. At this point, I don't know what me and Amari are, but it feels good every time he tells me that. I pulled away from our hug and then gave him a smile. When I exited the room, my phone had rung. I saw that it was Erica again so this time I answered.

"Hello," I said as I pressed the button to the elevator.

"Girllllll," she dragged, "I have some drama to tell you!"

I smiled because it had been a while since we knew someone's business.

"Oooo get to telling. Damn, the elevator is here, so my phone is going to cut off," I said to her. Right when I was about to tell her that I would call her back when I got off the elevator, she spoke.

"Well, I'll tell you when you get home. I called ya Nana, and she said that I could spend the night. I hope that's okay with you."

I was excited because it had been a while since we had hung out. I told Erica that I would see her when I got home. Mr. Harry had given me cab money, so after flagging down a cab

towards home, I just sat in the back of the car and thought
about what she had to tell me.

***

I used my keys to open the front door to the apartment
and was met with the smell of food. My stomach started to
growl because I hadn't eaten since school lunch. At the
hospital, Amari tried to offer me his food, but I didn't want
that hospital made sandwich. Plus, now that he had an
appetite, I preferred that he ate his own food. I took my snow-
covered boots off and then left them at the door. After taking
off my coat and putting it in the hallway closet, I made my way
to the kitchen because I knew that's where Nana was. I was
shocked to find Erica in the kitchen, helping her. At her house,
she didn't even help her own mother cook, so it was surprising
to see her helping my grandmother.

"Hey, y'all." I greeted.

"Y'all?" Nana corrected me.

"Sorry, mam, hey Nana and Erica."

She had just started letting me slide with greeting her using
the word, hey, and there I was pushing it by adding y'all to it.

"Gone head Erica. Wash your hands, and then you can
go. Thank you for keeping me company while she was gone."
Erica smiled and then washed her hands in the kitchen sink.

"How is he?" Nana asked me about Amari.

"He's good. He gets discharged tomorrow, so that's big."

"Yes, that's good."

Nana gave me her warm smile. I waited for Erica to finish washing her hands before I made my way towards my bedroom.

Walking past, I peeked my head into the living room to say hello to Mr. Harry. He was stretched out onto the couch sleeping. I never understood why he just didn't go lay in Nana's bed. I don't know what image they were trying to preserve, but I already knew the deal between the two of them. Mr. Harry was my unspoken grandfather I just wished that Nana would stop playing the he's just a good friend game with him. I opened my room door, and after Erica walked in after me, she closed it behind her. Jumping straight into it, I had to know what was going on.

"So, go. Who you got the scoop on?" I asked as I started to come out of my clothes.

Me and Erica got undressed in front of one another all of the time. So, I wasn't shy as I pulled my uniform from my body and replaced the clothes with some loungewear.

"Okay, soooooo…" she cut her eyes at me.

"Get on with it." I pushed.

"Guess who's pregnant?"

My eyes opened wide as I looked at her. She didn't look pregnant. Hell, I didn't even know what pregnant looked like.

"Ohhhh, hell no. It's not me."

She quickly said. She must have been reading my mind.

"I know y'all better watch that GODDAM language!"

I heard Nana say. She must have been in her room. That's the only way she could have heard us. I put my finger over my lips to silence Erica from finishing the story.

"Sorry, mam!" I called out.

"Mmmm hmmm," Nana grunted.

I heard footsteps, and then a few moments after that, I heard a Tyler Perry play running.

"Okay, go ahead and finish the story."

I said to Erica when I knew that the coast was clear.

I took a seat on my bed as she quickly changed into her pajamas and then took a seat next to me.

"Sooo Brandi is pregnant," Erica said.

I just rolled my eyes because it was expected. Brandi was the biggest pop (hoe) that I knew. She didn't care who she messed with. Moving how she did, you were bound to get caught out there.

"Well, that's not surprising," I said with a shrug.

"Oh, but it is... she's pregnant by King."

"What?" I asked.

Now my interest was peaked. To my knowledge, she was messing with G. I didn't get how she could have been pregnant by his brother.

"How is she pregnant by King when she was messing around with G," I added.

The situation really wasn't making any sense to me.

"Soooo, here's the thing. She was never messing with G. G said that she was always messing with King. She got pregnant, and she asked G for some abortion money because when she asked King, he told her hell no. G told me that he told her that he wasn't giving her shit either so he took the money from King since the baby was his responsibility to begin with. He gave the money to Brandi and guess what the fuck she did with it?"

This had to be the same money that King thought I stole, I thought to myself. I remained quiet because I was waiting for her to finish.

"She used the money to go shopping," Erica said and then started laughing.

"Oh, wow," I said dryly.

I found no interest in the situation. I had got accused of lifting that same money that had been stolen. Stolen from his brother at that, and I'm pretty sure that I got shot at for it

too. Erica stopped laughing when she realized that I wasn't
interested. After she asked me what was wrong, I explained to
her how King had accused me of stealing that money.

"Damn, Dee Dee. You think that's why he shot at
y'all?" she asked.

"I mean, I think so."

I didn't say anything else about what she had just told me
because, in my head, it still wasn't making sense. If you ask
me, I think that Brandi is pregnant with G's baby and that G
stole the money from King to try and make Brandi go and get
an abortion. I think that his plan backfired when she took that
money and went shopping. The only reason why I think that
Erica had this big ass story to tell is that G probably decided
to feed her that bullshit to preserve whatever relationship they
have left.

"Aye Erica, be careful with G, okay?"

"Girl ain't nobody worried about him." She said
dismissively.

Although I knew that she was indeed worried about him, I left
the topic alone. For the rest of the weekend, we watched
movies and then did some homework. Every few minutes me
and Amari were texting. We would have been on the phone if
Erica wasn't over. I urged that he should have still called, but
he insisted that I enjoy my girl time. This is why I loved him

because he was understanding. The whole weekend I wondered if I should tell Erica what Amari had told me about the beef between him and King.

Deciding against it, I kept my mouth shut. I enjoyed my weekend with my girl, but I can honestly say that I was excited when she had left that Sunday. All weekend I yearned to hear Amari's voice and her being over was interfering with that. I still didn't know what me and him were. I didn't want Erica thinking that it was something that it wasn't. Nana and Mr. Harry had left out to take Erica home. I was asked why I didn't want to go, and I simply told them that my stomach was bothering me. It wasn't all a lie I was experiencing cramps, but they weren't as bad as I made them out to be.

I ended up falling asleep on Amari on the phone. I didn't realize that I was even tired until I got nice and comfortable under my blanket. Somewhere in the middle of my sleep, I ended up waking because I heard Nana dragging her slippers around the apartment. I figured that she was back from taking Erica home. When I looked at my cellphone, I saw that it was seven in the evening and the phone was still connected. I put the phone to my ear and heard what sound like a shooting game in the background.

"Hello," I whispered into the phone.
I cleared my throat because I sounded like a little boy.

"You up, shawty?"

I smiled. Amari had stayed on the phone while I was sleeping.

"You know you could have hung up? Right?"

I put the phone on my shoulder as I fixed my headscarf that was starting to come off.

"Nah, it was nice having you on the phone. It feels like you here or something. I started playing the game once ya ass started snoring, though…"

I chuckled because I know damn well that I don't snore.

"I do not snore Amari," I said as I rolled my eyes.

"Well, I guess it's a bear in ya room or something."

"Deanna! Are you up?"

I heard Nana yell from outside of my room. Instantly I heard her feet getting closer to my door.

"I gotta go," I whispered to Amari just before I hung up.

As soon as I put my cellphone onto my bed, Nana pushed my door open.

"Here, this done came in the mail for you."

Nana tossed a big padded manila envelope onto my bed. The weight from whatever was inside hit my knee.

"Thanks, Nana."

"I don't know why ya mother sent anything when she's supposed to be down here next month for ya birthday. I swear

if she doesn't show her face, I'ma stick my foot so far up her ass…"

Nana continued to mumble as she made her way out of my room. I looked at the envelope and saw that there was no return address. Knowing that my mother was quick to drop anything in the mail for me, I just shrugged it off and then ripped open the big envelope.

My breathing started to pick up when I saw my diary. My first diary, the one that I thought I had lost. I flipped it from the front cover to the back cover repeatedly because I couldn't believe it. I took my fingertips and then graced over the pink ink that was carved into the composition notebook that read Dear Diary. Where the hell did I leave this, and how did it get here? I thought to myself as I started to flip through the pages. I smiled as I skimmed over my memories: the good, the bad and the ugly. I had been through so much drama within the year that it was refreshing to be coming out on the other side of it finally. In the middle of my book, a couple of pages were ripped out. I ran my hand across the ripped pages. I didn't remember ripping them out, so I was confused.

I flipped to the back of the book. Tears started to come down my eyes as I read…

Lil Mama,

You left this shit in my car. Funny how God works like that right? Well, I know by now you must know that I read all this shit. Now I'm just sitting here thinking... what to do with you. Not only did you steal money from me, but you were playing me. This whole time you had something going on with that little nigga Amari. Well, cool. I'll just chalk that up as a lessoned learned. Ya little young ass had a hold on me. A good one too but that shit is done. I hate you...

I wiped the tears from my eyes as I looked at the hand-drawn crown that was at the bottom of the page. Without a doubt, in my mind, I knew that the sender of this package had to be no other than King. I didn't even know how he knew where I lived. That made me feel so unsafe. I leaped up from my bed and then put my old diary inside of my bottom drawer. After throwing the envelope, it came in inside of my room garbage, I got back under my blanket. I needed to go back to sleep and just regroup the next day.

January 13th, 2008

Lately, my nerves have been bad. Rightfully I had all reason to feel that way. I still didn't know how King knew where I lived. Now, when I left school and traveled to the train, I looked over my shoulder. The last test I had I damn near flunked, which wasn't like me. I was distracted. Luckily, Mr. Rose let me have an immediate makeup test without informing Nana. I'm pretty sure that everyone around me could see how much stress I was under. I knew that if no one else saw it, Amari did. After the day that I had today, I really just want to blink my eyes and get graduation over with. I want to hurry up and to get to high school. I want to start over…

"Yo Shawty, what's up with you? You been staring at the wall for the past ten minutes."

I heard what Amari was saying to me I just didn't feel like responding. I was out of it. *How does he know where I live?* I questioned myself.

"Hello?" He nudged my arm, which broke me out of my trance.

"Hmm?" I asked although I had heard what he said.

"What's good with you?"

By the time I had turned to face him, tears were welled in my eyes. My bottom lip quivered. I blew out a sharp breath to try and get myself together before the rest of our classmates noticed.

"Deanna…"

His brown eyes went soft when he whispered my name to me. He held sympathy in them, and for a minute, I saw him for who he truly was, a young boy. The façade that he put on for the outside world was gone as he gazed me in my eyes.

"Why are you about to cry?" he whispered to me.

"Ohhhh Mr. Gildan you and Ms. Dixon must want to teach the class today hmmm—"

"Shut upppppppp," Amari hissed, cutting Mr. Rose off.

"Urm... excuse me?" Mr. Rose asked as he put the cap on the dry erase marker in his hand.

The entire class stopped what they were doing and then gave their attention to the center of the classroom. I made eye contact with Erica, and her eyes were wide open. We always clowned on talking crazy to teachers but none of us had never done it.

"Oh, Mr. Gildan out of my classroom."

"Aight... I have been put the fuck out of better."
Amari rose from his seat and then snatched his backpack off of the back of his chair. I stood, quickly put on my book bag, and then followed him.

"Ms. Dixon, this will not end well for you."
Mr. Rose said to me just before I let the classroom door closed behind me. Once we were in the hallway, there was an awkward silence. I don't know why I followed him out of the classroom but I just did.

February 6th, 2008

Since walking out of Mr. Rose's class, a lot has changed. For starters, Nana almost made a new butthole for me when she found out that I had walked out of class. The only thing that saved me was the simple fact that Amari had once saved me. She knew that the boy was troubled. Anyone at first glance could see that. She also knew that my heart was big and that I was not going to let him be alone when he was defending me.

When I had reached home that day, Mr. Rose had already called. After pleading my case and then getting off of the hook the next day when I went to school, I had to apologize for disrupting the class the day prior. Once I apologized, Mr. Rose agreed to have Amari and me back in his class. His only stipulation was that we don't fail any exams for the rest of the quarter. I knew that I could do that and Amari was smart as hell so I knew that he could too. We were a month and on track with our courses. For the first time in a long time, I actually enjoyed school. My grades were good, my boyfriend's grades were good and his health was good. Yes, I said boyfriend. On my birthday me and Amari made it official...

"Dee Dee, here!" Erica said eagerly, "open my gift." She added as she jumped up and down.

"Ughhh E, I told you that I didn't want any gifts." I sighed as I took the gift bag out of her hand.

As usual, I was the only one not dressed in uniform because it was my special day. This year I wanted to pass on the ritual that we had of opening presents during our lunch period, but I could already see that Erica was not going for that. I pulled the tissue paper out of the top of the bag and then pulled a shirt out of the bag. Glitter started to fall from the shirt which caused me to move my legs out of the way so that the gold flakes wouldn't get onto my jeans. *Dejavu,* I thought as I watched the glitter fall from the shirt. It reminded me of the gift I had gotten from Shells the year prior. Shaking thoughts of that bozo from my head, I unfolded the shirt and then held it out in front of me so that I could read what it said.

The black long-sleeved T-shirt had my name on the front in glitter along with shooting stars on it. I smiled brightly and then thanked Erica for the gift. After we shared a quick hug, I folded the shirt and then put it back into the gift bag.

"Who's next! Who's next?" I said excitedly. Most things didn't excite me at all, but because my friends were excited to give me gifts, I felt like I had to share the same joy with them.

"Well, I ain't got you nothing for real… so, ima just take you to Mc Donald's after school and you can get what you want." Valentine said with a smile. We had two McDonald's near our school.

"I'm not walking to the one all the way by the train," I stated as I crossed my arms over my chest.

"You're such a brat. Na sis we gone go to the other one since it's closer to us. Yo Ah, get ya girl man she's so spoiled." Valentine said the ending to Amari as he playfully rolled his eyes.

Amari rolled his big brown eyes my way. As our eyes connected, I smiled.

"Here, shawty."

He handed me an envelope.

"You tried giving me a letter last year you at it again now?" I asked with a raised eyebrow.

I pushed my hair towards my back and then ripped it open. The front of the birthday card had a dog with a birthday hat on. I opened the card and ignored the typed birthday message when I noticed his handwriting.

Do you want to be my girl?

| | **yes**

| | **no**

I smiled brightly and then fixed my face like I was in deep thought. Out the corner of my eye, I could see that Amari was looking at me. He held a brief sadness in his eyes. Once I noticed it, I figured that I wouldn't make him wait any longer. I dug around in my Baby Phat bookbag until I pulled a pen from one of the pockets. I checked the yes box and then closed the card and handed it back to him.

I saw him breathe out a sigh before he took a look at my answer. The corners of his mouth turned upward once he read my response.

"You sure?" He asked me as he patted my birthday card in his hand.

"I wouldn't have checked it if I weren't."
Amari stood from his seat and then gently kissed me on the cheek quickly before one of the teachers in the lunchroom could see.

"My dad is coming in town for my birthday, and so is my mom, you want to meet them?" I asked.
Both of my parents had already heard all of the great things about Amari. Nana held his name high ever since he saved me. I was nervous about them meeting him in person, but besides now being my boyfriend, he was my very best friend. The meeting was going to have to happen sooner or later.

"Oooo... I don't know, shawty. What happens if they don't like me or something."

Amari never cared about what other people thought of him, so to hear his concern in what my parents thought shocked me.

"They are going to love you," I assured him as I rubbed the back of his hand gently.

"Pshhh," he made a sound with his mouth, "Yea, only cause I took a couple of hot ones for you."

"And you did that because you love me, and they will see that."

He shook his head up and down to agree with me and then clasped his hands together.

"Aight shawty. When and where do you want me to meet them?"

"Ummmm, this weekend."

I didn't even clear this whole meet and greet with Nana, yet I was locking in dates.

"I'll keep you posted with the rest of the details once I find them out." I quickly added before he could respond to me.

A piece of me was iffy on inviting Amari over to my house, especially since I knew that King knew where I lived. I still didn't tell him about my old book showing up to my house from King. When I think about it, he doesn't even know that I write in a diary. He might think I'm childish because of it.

"What's good with you, shawty?" Amari snapped his fingers into my face.

I blinked twice and then focused in on him.

"Nothing."

He screwed his face up before he responded.

"You just zoned out, but there's nothing wrong...
okay."

I could tell that he was annoyed at me keeping him out
of my thoughts, but to me, it was for his safety. King had
already shot him once, and he came out on top of it. If it
happened a second time, I didn't think that King would let him
survive it.

"Let me know about this weekend, okay?"
Amari said to me before he gently kissed my cheek and then
walked out. The lunch period was done, and we didn't share
the same class after lunch. For the rest of the day, I sat lost in
my classes, wondering if and how I would pull the weekend
off.

February 9th, 2008

King is one less thing that I have to worry about, and I'm
grateful for it. The meeting with Amari and my parents went
smooth like I knew it would. At this point I'm so ready for
graduation, we're so ready for graduation...

I snatched all of my stuffed animals off of my bed and then tossed them into my closet. I knew damn well that Nana wouldn't allow Amari into my room, but during the tour of our two-bedroom apartment, I didn't want him to see them on my bed. I heard our buzzer going off and I knew that it had to either be my dad or Amari. My mother was already in the living room with Nana and Mr. Harry. Being that it was a small birthday celebration for me, I was expecting my cousin Rayne to come over with my aunt Mecca as well.

Knock, Knock

The door slowly opened.

"Hey, baby girl."

My dad walked over to me slowly with his arms out for a hug. I hugged him tightly because it had been a while since I saw him.

"Hi, daddy!" I said excitedly as we embraced.

It felt good being in the arms of my father. The girl in me grew teary-eyed as I thought of everything that I had encountered in the past year. I needed this hug from my dad. I didn't realize how much he had needed it from me until I went to pull back and he pulled me tighter into our hug. Because of his short height, my head was almost lying on his shoulder.

"Awwww, Dee Dee, I worry about you so much." He admitted.

He kissed the top of my head several times before he broke our embrace. He held onto my arms as he took a look at me.

"Look at you, my girl. You're getting soooo big."
He sniffled, and moments later, the mist in his eyes faded.

"So, what do you want for your birthday?" He asked. The buzzer went off again, and nervous butterflies floated around in my stomach.

"Daddy... I have a friend coming over today, the same friend that saved me. What I want for my birthday is for you to like him because I really like him."
I said everything in one breath. My dad's button nose crinkled at the end of my statement.

"Pleaseeeee, daddy."

"Dee Dee, your company is here!" I heard Nana call out.

"Alright dammit," my dad shrugged his shoulders, "you're growing up, man."
He opened my room door and then held it open for me to walk in front of him.

I moved one of my curls out of my face before we walked into the living room. I smiled when I saw Amari taking off his coat and handing it to Mr. Harry so that it could be put into our closet. A gift bag with balloons tied to the handle sat on the couch near my mother.

"Mommy, what you got me?" I asked her as soon as I got fully into the living room.

"This isn't my gift for you. This is from your little friend."

I looked at Amari and then smiled.

"You get gifts?" I asked.

"You gotta do special things for special people, right?" He said with a smirk.

I blushed, and the silence in the room made me clear my throat before I formally introduced everyone in the room to Amari. He gave hugs to my mother and Nana, he shook Mr. Harry hand and then went to shake my dad's hand. Their handshake was longer than the one that Amari had shared with Mr. Harry.

"I wanna thank you, young man, for saving my baby girl."

I smiled at my dad's statement.

"It was really nothing."

Amari was so nonchalant when it came to him taking bullets, and I hated but loved it at the same time.

Nana excused herself out of the living room to check on the food that was cooking in the kitchen.

"Can I open this now or—"

"Girl, if you don't wait until we finish eating so that you can open all of your gifts together." My mother interrupted me.

"Come on, y'all the food is ready."
Nana peeked her head into the living room and said to us. Together we all made our way into the dining room. Amari pulled out a chair for me and on the inside, I almost died. I don't mean to diss him or anything but he was showing how much of a gentleman he could be.

"Awww Mike, why the hell you can't pull out my damn chair." My mom complained to my dad.

"Chrissy cut it out, man. Can I make it to that end of the table to pull your seat out first before you get to complaining? See this all you did when we were married." My father said jokingly.
He walked to the end of the table and then pulled the chair out for my mother to sit. Mr. Harry pulled out Nana's chair for her to sit. Before I got comfortable in my seat, the buzzer started to ring.

"Dee Dee, go and get that bell, please," Nana said to me.
I sighed under my breath of course because Nana would have slapped me right in front of my company.

"Okay, mam."

Amari looked like he wanted to go with me, but my family had already started engaging in conversation with him that kept him planted at the table.

"Dee Dee is a good kid and has always been one. So, although she's fifteen, I think she should be allowed to have a little boyfriend," I heard my mother say before my dad and Nana chipped in.

When I got to the hallway, I pressed the buzzer to let whoever was ringing it downstairs in, but instead of hearing the door unlocking, I heard static.

"Ughhhh," I groaned when I realized that I would have to walk down the two flight of stairs to let who had to be my aunt Mecca and cousin Rayne in.

"I gotta go downstairs, y'all the buzzer is broken." I said as I sucked my teeth and grabbed my house keys off of the key rack.

I left the front door open and then made my way downstairs. I couldn't see through the gated door, but I pulled it open anyway. Before I could even think King pushed me into the lobby of my building. He put his hand over my mouth and then pushed me into the wall behind me.

"Now what should I do with you, little Miss Deanna? Hmm?"

I gulped hard, and then tears welled into my eyes. What the hell is he doing here? I wondered to myself. I tried pleading with him with my eyes but he wasn't letting up. He stroked the side of my face with the back of his hand and then traveled that hand down to my neck. He applied pressure to my throat. It wasn't like he was choking me; he was more so taunting me.

"Happy birthday Lil Mama." He whispered into my ear before gently kissing me on the cheek.

The sound of someone putting a key into the steel door caused him to back away from me. I was surprised to see who it was because I didn't think that she still had a key to Nana's house. At one point, all of Nana's kids had a key to her apartment for safety reasons but once Mr. Harry came into the picture, Nana went collecting her keys. My aunt Mecca was the first to walk through the door, followed by my cousin Rayne and my uncle Tron. Rayne's father had been locked up since Rayne and I was little girls. I didn't even know when he had come home but it felt good seeing him.

"What the hell is going on here?" Aunt Mecca asked with a raised eyebrow.
I knew that my curls probably look disheveled. I looked at Rayne with watery eyes. She was the only one I ever told about the diary coming back to the house. She knew about the

pregnancy scare, and she knew about King's hand problem. She quickly looked at King and then a coldness filled her eyes.

"Daddy, this boy hurt Dee Dee."

Without asking Rayne to repeat herself, my uncle, Tron, made his way to King. I saw that King attempted to reach for something in his waist but my uncle had him choked off the floor before that could even happen.

"You was tryna shoot me, lil nigga?" Uncle Tron asked.
I saw King's face turning blue as his eyes bulged out of his head.

"Mecca, take the girls upstairs! Don't even tell anyone that I'm home yet let me handle him first." Uncle Tron said to my aunt.
He never let lose of King and never took his eyes off of him either.

"Let's go y'all." Aunt Mecca said and grabbed both me and Rayne by the arms.

We all climbed the two flights of stairs, and when we made it to the second level, Aunt Mecca told Rayne and me to have a seat on the staircase that was leading to the level above us.

"Dee Dee, let me fix your hair." She said as she ran her fingers through my curls. "He looks too old for you baby girl.

117

Older men are dangerous, it seems alluring but it's not what you want. You don't want the rush that they give you. It may seem appealing but that kind of rush is never good for your heart."

Tears built in my eyes as I listened to my aunt speak.

"Who I want is in the house right now with everyone. He took bullets for me, auntie. There's nobody I could ever want but him."

Aunt Mecca smiled at me and then rubbed my cheek. She wiped away my tears before she spoke.

"Your uncle took bullets for me before, but that's a story for another time. Your little friend from downstairs will be taken care of so you enjoy your birthday celebration with the people that care about you most."

She held her arms out, "come give me a hug. Both of y'all."

Me and Rayne stood to hug my aunt. "Y'all fast tail asses are gonna give me a heart attack."

My aunt Mecca knew all about Rayne and the boys she would talk to. She was that cool aunt but within reason. We all got ourselves together before we walked back into the house.

"This is our secret, Deanna," my aunt whispered to me as we walked down the long hallway in the apartment.

"I know auntie, thank you. Now come and meet him." I said with a smile referring to Amari.

I enjoyed the rest of my birthday celebration with the weight of King lifted from my spirits. School was great, and home was amazing. So much, that I was looking forward to wrapping up middle school and then moving on to the next chapter.

June 26th, 2008

It was my first time wearing a strapless dress, so for the most part of the day, I kept catching my self pulling at the bandage part. My graduation dress was orange, hot pink and had splashes of yellow. I wore hot pink heels. My mom had to do a lot of convincing with Nana for me to wear the short five-inch heel. Momma had taken me to the Dominicans to get a blowout and in my hair, I wore a silver clip. I was stepping over the threshold. Saying goodbye to middle and hello to high school. Because of all of the weekend study courses that I had taken at Bedford Academy, I was going there for high school. The principal of the school pulled Amari in with no problem after seeing the story about his shooting on the local news. It was already prearranged that Amari would be joining their basketball team in his freshman year.

Erica applied to a high school that was closer to her house. Every now then she tells me that she speaks to G. The only reason why she tells me that they still speak is because he needs an outlet. He's dealing with a lot right now. His brother has been missing for four months and he's about to be a new father. It turns out that Brandi's baby was his after all. As I sat in the auditorium chair in my cap and gown, I briefly listened to the speech that my principal was saying. We had already walked on stage to retrieve our awards. The ceremony was closing up and he was our last speaker.

"As you leave this chapter in your life, look forward to what's to come. The last three years prepared you for this very moment. Don't be discouraged in September when you all are walking through new doors. Some of these faces may travel with you throughout your life and others were just for the moment. Never forget your fundamentals. What you were taught in this school should always travel with you. What your peers have taught you throughout these three years should always travel with you. Without further ado, I present to you the class of 2008. Go ahead y'all… throw them caps up."

The entire graduating class threw their caps up. The girls' gold caps mixed in with the boys' blue ones. In the next row to the right of me was the boys' side. Me and Amari locked eyes. I smiled brightly as I caught a gold cap that I'm sure probably didn't even belong to me. He smiled back at me as he caught a blue one. Amari blew me a kiss which made me blush. I caught it and then placed it on my cheek. I was so ready for the next chapter. High school here I come… sorry, high school here WE come. As long as my best friend/boyfriend and I stay true to one another, I think we will be okay.

THE END

There was a little bit of Deanna Dixon in all of us.

Follow C. Wilson on social media

Instagram: @authorcwilson

Facebook: @CelesteWilson

Join my reading group on Facebook: Cecret Discussionz

Follow my reading group on Instagram:
@CecretDiscussionz

Twitter: @Authorcwilson_

C. Wilson

~~~~~~

Tell me what you think of this story in a customer review.

Thank you,

-xoxo-

C. Wilson

Made in the USA
Columbia, SC
09 February 2025